LUCKY SUIT

LAUREN BLAKELY

ALSO BY LAUREN BLAKELY

Big Rock Series

Big Rock

Mister O

Well Hung

Full Package

Joy Ride

Hard Wood

One Love Series

The Sexy One

The Only One

The Hot One

The Knocked Up Plan

Come As You Are

The Heartbreakers Series

Once Upon a Real Good Time

Once Upon a Sure Thing

Once Upon a Wild Fling

Sports Romance

Most Valuable Playboy

Most Likely to Score

Lucky In Love Series

Best Laid Plans

The Feel Good Factor

Nobody Does It Better

Unzipped

Always Satisfied Series

Satisfaction Guaranteed

Instant Gratification

Overnight Service

Never Have I Ever

Special Delivery

The Gift Series

The Engagement Gift

The Virgin Gift (coming soon)

The Exclusive Gift (coming soon)

Standalone

Stud Finder

The V Card

Wanderlust

Part-Time Lover

The Real Deal

Unbreak My Heart

The Break-Up Album

21 Stolen Kisses

Out of Bounds

Birthday Suit

The Dating Proposal

The Caught Up in Love Series

Caught Up In Us

Pretending He's Mine

Playing With Her Heart

Stars In Their Eyes Duet

My Charming Rival

My Sexy Rival

The No Regrets Series

The Thrill of It

The Start of Us

Every Second With You

The Seductive Nights Series

First Night (Julia and Clay, prequel novella)

Night After Night (Julia and Clay, book one)

After This Night (Julia and Clay, book two)

One More Night (Julia and Clay, book three)

A Wildly Seductive Night (Julia and Clay novella, book 3.5)

The Joy Delivered Duet

Nights With Him (A standalone novel about Michelle and Jack)

Forbidden Nights (A standalone novel about Nate and Casey)

The Sinful Nights Series

Sweet Sinful Nights

Sinful Desire

Sinful Longing

Sinful Love

The Fighting Fire Series

Burn For Me (Smith and Jamie)

Melt for Him (Megan and Becker)

Consumed By You (Travis and Cara)

The Jewel Series

A two-book sexy contemporary romance series

The Sapphire Affair

The Sapphire Heist

LUCKY SUIT

ABOUT

I'm breaking up with set-ups. No more "can I introduce you to my son, nephew, grandson, the butcher, the guy down the street who mows my lawn." Machines know what's best, and I'll rely on the great dating algorithms of the web to find the ideal man, thank you very much.

Soon enough, it looks like I've found him — his nickname is Lucky Suit, and he's hilarious, quick-witted and full of heart. But when I finally get together with him in person, I have the distinct feeling I've met him before.

Turns out there's more to our meeting than I had thought, and when we discover what truly brought us together, all bets are off.

1

Kristen

I'll tell Grams as soon as I see her.

I'll break the news to her and then explain why my new plan is the logical one.

First, though, I adjust the aperture on my telescope, and one of my favorite sights comes into view. The Andromeda Galaxy is such a show-off tonight, and nothing beats that billion-star galaxy. It's all yummy and triumphant in the sky, as if it's saying to the Milky Way, "I'm coming to get you in four and a half billion years."

I'm savoring the view, because the night sky rocks, when I hear footsteps.

"Tell me what?"

I startle, yank my eyes away from the telescope, and stare at my grandma, who's snuck out on the balcony we share, since her condo is right next to mine. "Were you here the whole time?"

She quirks up her lips in a *gotcha* grin. She is so good at that. She could teach a master class in giving that grin to grown granddaughters.

"Long enough to hear you had something to tell me."

"I said that out loud?" I shove my glasses up the bridge of my nose.

She parks her hands on her hips, still fabulous in her skinny jeans at seventy-five. Dear God, may I please have her *genes*, with a capital *G*? "Yes. So . . . spill. What do you have to tell me? You car-napped my Mustang and did donuts in the 7-Eleven lot last night? You borrowed my new Louboutins without asking? Or you're selling your half of this Key Biscayne duplex because you feel guilty about the way you cramp my style?"

"One, you don't own Louboutins. You shop for shoes at Payless, and don't deny it. Two, it's a Corvette, not a Mustang. You can't trick me on that count either. And three, I can totally handle the way I cramp your style." I add a saucy finger snap for effect.

"You take after me way too much," she says, laughing. Her tone softens, the sass stripped away. "Seriously, what do you need to tell me?"

I take a deep breath. "Sit."

"Uh-oh."

I point to the table where I left my tablet. I

swipe across the screen, opening it to an email I wrote earlier.

Dear Mr. O'Leary,

Please accept this letter as notice that I will be resigning from our third date, effective immediately.

Thank you for the compliments, the cup of coffee (really, that was some seriously great joe), and the chance to chat for forty-six minutes after we learned how to coagulate cheese. You are a fine man and will likely prove to be an exemplary partner for a mate someday.

If I can do anything to help with your transition in finding and training my replacement, please let me know. I feel it's only right to tell you that I am officially 100 percent done with IRL dating. So it is with utmost honesty that I say, it's not you. It's definitely me.

Sincerely,

Kristen Leonard

I look up to see the side-eye.

Wait. That's not the side-eye. That's the you-can't-be-serious eye.

Then it morphs into the doubled-over-in-laughter hoot.

And I maintain my best oh-so-stoic face.

"What?" I feign confusion. "Is it because I didn't spell out IRL? He'll know what it means, right? Was I too internet-y? That's totally possible." I play up my innocence, like little ole me made an etiquette faux pas. "Sometimes I get caught up in the lingo. I can just spell it out. You want me to spell it out?"

She fans her face like she can restore the oxygen she lost from her laughing fit. "Training a replacement? It was only two dates."

"Two dates too many." I straighten my shoulders. "And I thought I should be considerate in sending a breakup letter. Establish a new standard, if you will."

One eyebrow climbs. She studies me quizzically, scanning my long brown hair, my green eyes, my freckles as if she's never seen me before, then her eyes narrow. "Wait. I'm onto you. Did you simply google resignation letters?"

I let my smile spread. It's not often I can pull a fast one on her, and it's glorious. "Gotcha."

Her lips quirk up, and she wags a finger. "You little prankster. I thought for sure you were going to send this."

"Please. You know me better. I'm going to send a super-short email along the lines of *Thanks, but I feel we're not the best fit.*"

She wipes imaginary sweat from her forehead. "You had me going."

I blow on my fingernails. "I still got it. I learned from the best."

"I have taught you well, and I will now take all the credit. Also, I can't believe you didn't like Henry. Why not?"

"Look, I know your friend Betty thought we'd be great together, but I just didn't feel like he and I had anything in common. He actually *liked* the cheese-making class. I don't want to make cheese. I want it served to me. Who has time to make food from scratch when it's just as easy to order it or, gee, I dunno, *buy it*?"

"Fine, so you didn't both like making cheese. But you truly didn't connect on anything?"

I shake my head. "We didn't have a chance to learn if we did. All he talked about was the cheese. And then the coffee. Nothing more interesting. Nothing like black holes or the meaning of the universe. Or perhaps why certain cult classic TV shows aren't streaming online—like *Cupid* with Jeremy Piven, which is arguably the best show ever canceled before its time."

"And every time you mention it, I want to see it more and more. We could try to hunt down DVDs. Did you check eBay?"

"I've tried. Believe you me, I have tried. It's harder to track down than buried treasure." I sigh. "But see, this is my point. It's such a better conversation topic than cheese."

"What about Sandy's grandson, Matthew? The one from the pickling class? He seemed like the type you could discuss anything with."

"The trouble with Matthew is the whole time

during the pickling class he kept telling me about his job."

"It's normal to discuss your career with a date. I'm sure you mention your work sometimes," she says gently, as if she's talking to someone who has no clue about dating, men, and human interaction.

But I do indeed have some clue. I've been on enough dates and enough bad ones to know what I want and don't want, thank you very much. I want to leave my work as an alternative fuel scientist at the lab, and call me crazy, but some professions don't lend themselves to small talk.

"Grams. He works at a funeral home. He told me all about embalming people . . . during a *carrot pickling class*."

She tuts. "Fine, so he needs some work on social skills. Who doesn't?"

"Plus, pickled carrots? Ewww. Just eww."

"What about Sally's grandson Freddie? We set up you on the glassblowing date. That seemed fun."

I shoot her a stern look. "Glassblowing, Grams. Don't you remember what I told you? It was like a nonstop slapstick night of inappropriate jokes, and none were even funny. I love you and all of your efforts to set me up, but here's the thing: these in-person matches don't work on me. I'm evidently immune to matchmaking IRL."

She smiles hopefully. "Maybe you just haven't met the one yet."

I sketch air quotes. "There is no 'the one.' There are many. But the trouble is meeting men in these real-life situations has a risk-to-reward ratio that's too high." I count off on my fingers. "I've gone to singles yoga classes, and I find nothing duller than *omm*ing my way through ninety minutes of mantras. I've attended wine tastings, even though I believe it's a conspiracy to convince us the beverage is amazing when, in fact, it tastes literally like dirt, and I even signed up for ballroom dancing, but I infinitely prefer fast-paced sports on wheels. And don't even get me started on Ping-Pong lessons."

"Ping-Pong lessons are an excellent way to meet a soul mate. You do know I met your grand-father, may he rest in peace, at Ping-Pong lessons."

"That was more than fifty years ago. You were twenty-one."

"Ping-Pong was fun then, and it's fun now." She gives me a coy little smile. "After all, there's a reason your mom was born when I was only twenty-two."

I blink, pause, process. "And now Ping-Pong is officially ruined forever."

"Your mom took Ping-Pong lessons too," she says, practically taunting me. "She took them when she was twenty-four, and voilà, you were born nine months later."

I arch one brow. "I'm feeling like Ping-Pong lessons are a euphemism for something. Call me crazy."

"I'm just saying, it's fun whacking a ball back and forth."

"And the double entendres continue. Which may explain why I don't care for it, and I don't want any unexpected side effects nine months after a game."

"Fine, fine. Shall I cast a wider net, then? Ask some of my friends at poker club? Or maybe in my water aerobics class?"

I slice a hand through the air. "I love you, but no. Setups and other randomly selected in-person dates rely too much on luck and chance and happenstance. Think about it. What are the true mathematical chances I'll meet a man who is at least eighty percent compatible with me—and that's my baseline—during Ping-Pong lessons?"

She rolls her eyes. "There's a good chance."

That's the problem. I'm at the point where I want *more* than a string of dates. I want the same thing everyone wants—a spark, a sizzle, and a person. A *someone* I like being with, sharing with, spending my days with.

But that starts with common ground.

And finding common ground requires a whole new strategy.

"From here on out, it's an algorithm and an algorithm-only world." I raise my arms like a high priestess. "I believe in the church of Google. I pray at the altar of machines and put my trust in artificial intelligence." I grab my tablet and click to a dating site. "That's why I signed up for an online dating service, allowing me a wider selection of potential dates and a more systematic approach. I've already chatted with a few men. Let me show you Jared." I click on the profile of a software developer with gray eyes and a square jaw.

She shudders. "Serial killer."

"Grams."

She shakes her head. "Mark my words. Those beady eyes."

Fine, maybe Jared and his little eyes aren't the best place to start. Clicking around, I find a profile of Porter, who's new to the site and looks promising. I read his note to me out loud. *"Good evening, Kristen. It's a pleasure to make your acquaintance. I was delighted by your profile and am tickled pink to know you enjoy piano, logarithmic functions, studying new sources for alternative energy, and the companionship of a good science book."*

She stares at me like I did, in fact, steal her prized car for a late-night joy ride. "He's clearly an ax murderer."

"How on earth could you say that?"

She points at the screen. "Porter is either an ax murderer or wears ladies' underwear."

Laughing, I shake my head. "He is not."

But now the idea's been planted in my head, and I'm not too fond of it. Neither the ax murderer nor the undies.

"Let's try one more." I swipe over to Wallace. "Look, he's perfect for me. He believes in the beauty of a well-formatted spreadsheet." I flutter my hand against my chest as if it's my beating heart. "Is there anything better than the behind-the-scenes functions baked into a spreadsheet?"

"Everything. Literally everything."

I hum thoughtfully, like I don't know it drives her crazy when I go full math geek on her. "I don't know. Spreadsheets are mega hot. I think I'll write back."

She grabs my wrist, her blue eyes tinged with genuine desperation. "He could be dangerous. Why don't we use a matchmaker instead?"

"Isn't that what we already did though?"

"I mean, an official matchmaker."

"Who does that anymore? Are we in *Fiddler on the Roof*?"

"No, but that's a damn good musical."

"True. That's one thing we can agree on. But listen, I'm confident I'll find someone online who shares my interests."

"Question-asking, troublemaking, and high levels of sarcasm?"

I smile. "I also enjoy beaches, museums, and urban art, thank you very much."

And, I'd like to find that certain someone who likes the same things. Who wants to learn from me, and who I can learn from. Someone to talk to.

Someone I can share my days and nights with.

Later, I send a simpler thanks-but-no-thanks letter to Henry, and he replies with a curt *same*, only solidifying my belief that I made the right choice.

* * *

The next morning when I open the door to my condo at Grams's knock, she quirks a brow then breathes a sigh of relief. "You survived the night, I see. Now please tell me Porter didn't lock you up in a supply closet."

"No, I locked him up. Would you mind coming inside and helping me remove the duct tape from his wrists?" I deadpan.

She narrows her eyes. "You are always trying to pull a fast one."

"Because you're always trying to be faster." I shoo her away. "Go see your friends, Grams. It's Sunday Funday and you have poker club and the repo car auction."

Her expression lights up, and she rubs her palms. "I do love seized cars. And how fabulous is your mother for finding me a new sale to check out?"

"She is most fabulous at taking an interest in our passions." My mom, I admit, is pretty freaking cool.

"If I'm lucky I can finally nab a Camaro there for Betty."

"Don't forget, if you come across a Bugatti, you better bid literally everything on it for me. Like, feel free to use my brother's rare baseball cards as collateral."

"Do you seriously think there are any Bugattis at police auctions?"

"Hope springs eternal."

She takes off, and on my way to the roller rink to work out—because skating equals killer cardio—I stop to grab a cup of coffee with my mom, updating her on Grams's ax murderer concerns.

"You know what your grams is like. Too many crime shows. Besides, you have pretty good radar when it comes to people. Just don't invite any men to your home, a back alley, a dark and deserted road, a public park, or any place with less than one hundred people. Oh, and be sure to text me before any dates with strangers so I'll know your whereabouts too."

"Oh yeah. Definitely. Want me to check in with you, too, every thirty minutes when I'm out on a date?"

Her green eyes, the same shade as mine, sparkle. "I would. Speaking of checking in, did Grams make it to the auction?"

I check my phone, nodding. "She says she's enjoying the view." I stare at her. "Your mom is a dirty bird."

2

Cameron

I like to imagine my life in montage moments.

If this were a movie, I'd get to skip the lazy slug of traffic I'm stuck in and magically appear at my destination.

Admittedly, I could have made a better effort to get to the car auction on time, but I'd been distracted when I left my South Beach hotel and spotted a pack of flamingos on the beach. Naturally, I had to take photos of them for my business partner and for my collection.

Of flamingo photos.

Yes, I have one now, because I like to snap pictures of cool things, pretty things, and weird things, and birds that stand on one leg qualify on all counts. Plus, I suspect the pic is about to become a business expense, since Lulu's unicorn avatar is flashing on my screen. In the interest of full disclosure, I did *not* set her avatar. She did. Everyone else just gets a name. Lulu gets a magical horse, and it's blinking at me, so I swipe my thumb across the screen and chat hands-free.

"Cameron!" Lulu greets me in exclamation points.

"Lulu!"

"I have an idea. Wait for it . . ." Pretty sure I know what's coming. "Flamingo-shaped chocolate."

I nod as I tap the gas, nudging the car forward. "Go ahead. Call me brilliant. Call me a fortune-teller."

"You are, but why would I call you a fortune-teller?"

"I knew that was what you were going to say."

"And how do I know you knew that?"

I smile. "You'll just have to trust me."

"But seriously. It's a great idea, and since you're in town working on the deal . . ."

"You want me to see if the chichi hotel near the Fontainebleau would carry them?"

"It's like we share a brain."

"That, and I've been working on a deal with them for the last week."

"We should definitely make the flamingo ones for them, don't you think?"

"A better idea there has never been."

"What if we do quirky animal-shaped chocolates that are themed for the different cities where you strike distribution deals?"

"Aren't animal crackers proof that animal-shaped food is, one, awesome, and two, profitable?"

She laughs. "Okay, I've convinced you, and you've convinced me. Let's do it."

"How about you make some samples, fly down here, and come with me to meet with them in person on Monday?"

"Fine, fine, twist my arm. I'll book a ticket for tonight."

"And we'll pitch them together tomorrow."

I say goodbye and will the traffic to move faster. Eventually it does, and I make it on time to the junkyard, where I park my rental and head over to say hello to Uncle Joe, who's studying a folder of papers while leaning against an old school bus. I fist-bump the man. "Silver Fox. What's up?"

He drops the papers to his side, giving me a stern stare. "It's about time. I'm not sure I'm going to save the old beat-up Ferrari for you anymore."

My eyes bulge. "You have a Ferrari today?"

His sky-blue eyes sparkle, crinkling at the corners, well-worn from the years. "Don't you want to know."

"Seriously? Are you messing with me?"

"What would you even do with a Ferrari? You live in Manhattan. You're only here a few times a year, yet you keep coming back to the junkyard like you're really going to buy some sweet, hot sports car and drive it down the Keys."

I square my shoulders as if I've truly taken offense to his comment. "I might very well do that someday."

He scoffs. "I bet on you *not* doing that."

"A man can dream, and I dream of buying a Ferrari and cruising over the Seven Mile Bridge to the edge of the Keys."

"I'm calling your bluff."

"Why don't you step on my dreams a little more?" I stick out my polished black wing tip and crush the toe against the ground like I'm squashing a bug. "Then maybe a little further. Just dig into my dream and destroy it."

He laughs, eyeing me up and down. "When you ditch those New York suits in favor of some *Miami Vice* duds to match that whole blue-eyed-blond thing, that's when I believe you'll buy one of the cars I'm auctioning, rather than only coming here to window-shop."

I shudder. "Salmon, puce, pink, and I do not get along. Also, nice to see you too."

A smile spreads nice and wide on his face, and he yanks me in for a big hug. My mom's older brother was integral to my life growing up here in Florida. I love the guy madly. "You have no idea how fun it is to give you a hard time."

"Oh, I have a bit of an idea, since you do it all the time."

He taps the side of the bus. Usually he

conducts the auction from the steps of the vehicle, megaphone in hand. "I need to review the list of goodies up for grabs. Lunch is on you today."

"Isn't it always?"

"That's what I like to hear."

I wave him off and head for the pack of car buyers, spotting a familiar face in the crowd, Jeanne. I chatted with her the last time I was here, and she's a hoot.

She's perched on an old Dodge, likely reviewing the list of items up for grabs today, with purple reading glasses low on her nose and a studious look on her weathered face. And she's wearing the least little-old-lady outfit I've ever seen —jeans and a basic black top. I imagine no elasticized waistbands of polyester have ever entered her home.

"Is this seat taken?"

She snaps up her gaze. "That depends on whether a handsome young man is going to park his butt on the hood of this car, or if some old fellow who smells like Vicks VapoRub will try to snag the coveted spot next to me."

"Definitely no Vicks VapoRub on me today, Jeanne. But young? I don't know. I'm pushing thirty-three."

She tuts. "Practically a boy-child."

I drop a kiss on her cheek, enjoying the faint scent of lilacs surrounding her. "What's shaking? I haven't seen you since that Mercury was up for grabs the other month."

She groans dramatically, clasping her cheeks. "Don't remind me. I lost out on that one, and I was dying for it."

"How many cars can you have, woman?"

She narrows her brows and wags a finger. "I have four, thank you very much. And it seems a downright sin not to have a fifth."

"Well, good thing you can make amends for that sin today."

"Indeed." She taps the list of items. "If I can snag the Camaro, I can fix it up and give it to my friend Betty."

"That's what you do with the cars?"

She smiles proudly. "It is. If I see any more of my girlfriends driving Buicks and Cadillacs, I will disown them. That's why I bid on the sports cars on their last legs then fix them up for my girls."

"Can I be your best friend when I'm seventy-five?"

She pats my leg. "Only if you play bridge, gin rummy, or poker."

I raise a hand. "All of the above."

"That so?"

I waggle my phone. "Online poker fiend at your service."

"We have lots to talk about, then."

"But first . . ." I glance at the school bus, where Joe is finishing his prep work, then whisper, "Why don't I let Joe know to give you some sugar when it comes to the Camaro?"

She clasps her hands together in prayer. "I'd

say I want to win fair and square, but we all know that's a bald-faced lie, so anything he can do to grease the wheels would be fantastic. I'd be willing to pay a little more than the opening bid."

"How much?"

She gives me a number.

"Let me see what I can do for you," I say with a wink, and I return to Joe. He raises his chin, glances at me, and scrubs a hand across his silvery beard. "You again? I'm telling you, Cam, you need to take action here. Less talk, more buying."

"I'll get to it."

He sighs heavily, shaking his head. "You always did spend too much time thinking. Everything had to be analyzed, considered, weighed. Even as a kid, you debated *Should I play with the Matchbox cars or the Legos? Let me weigh the pros and cons.*"

"Those were important choices. There is nothing wrong with thinking. It happens to be my . . . second-favorite activity."

Joe laughs, pointing at me. "Good one. And I agree on the first."

"Anyway, would you do me a solid? Any chance you can make sure the Camaro goes to a certain someone?" I tip my forehead toward Jeanne.

His eyes land on her, and he whistles low. "Babe alert."

I stare at him, flustered. "Babe? Isn't she about fifteen years older than you?"

"Are you an ageist when it comes to matters of the heart?"

"No way. I just thought you liked them the same age as you."

He hums his approval. "I am omnivorous when it comes to the ladies." He gestures to Jeanne. "What'll she pay for it?"

I give him Jeanne's price, and he says he'll consider it. I return to her. "No promises, but he'll see what he can do. Should be ready to start in five minutes."

Jeanne squeezes my arm. "You're a good man. How long are you in town this time?"

"Just a few more days. I have a couple meetings, then I take off for Vegas, then Chicago."

"You need to see the Wynwood Walls while you're here."

"I heard there were some new murals." The walls in that neighborhood teem with cool graffiti art.

"They're fantastic. Also, hello, online-poker fiend. What do you say to a game before this show gets on the road?"

Smiling, I take out my phone and tap open my poker app. "What's your screen name? I'm ready to take you down."

"HotRodLover."

I sputter. "That's your handle?"

She shrugs. "It fits me."

"A little double entendre there?"

"Shame on you," she says with a smirk. "And yours?"

I smile, eyeing my getup. Joe is right. Once a suit, always a suit. "LuckySuit."

We play a round on our phones. She beats me with an ace high, and then I even it up with a pair of kings. As the next hand is dealt, she looks my way out of the corner of her eye, asking as nonchalant as a cat padding into a library, "By the way, what ever happened to that woman you were seeing in New York?"

Briefly, I picture Isla, the clever investment banker I was seeing in Manhattan for a few months. She was pretty, witty, and chatty, all traits which attracted me, but eventually we ran out of topics to talk about. There are only so many conversations on the fluctuations in the financial markets that one man can bear listening to. Now, if she'd wanted to talk about the fine differences between rock music and indie pop, between Camus and Descartes, or between the work-to-live and the live-to-work approaches to life, we'd have shut every bar in the city down, chattering on well past the midnight hour.

"Things didn't work out with Isla. We didn't have too much in common. You know how it goes."

"You need someone who wants the same things. Who likes to think about the same things. You want someone who thinks."

"It's like you can read my mind. I believe that's

the key to dating success. Opposites don't attract, in my opinion. That's for magnets. With people, like attracts like. Also, your turn."

She plays one more hand, and I win with a trio of threes. She snaps her fingers. "But let's shoot a selfie for my Instagram feed. The boy who vanquished me in online poker."

"Thirty-two, Jeanne. Thirty-two."

She waves a hand. "Still a boy."

"Also, how the heck do you have an Instagram feed?"

"I don't let anything pass me by. Just because I'm seventy-five doesn't mean I'm not hip. I need someplace to post my cars."

She leans her head next to mine and snaps a shot of us, complete with wide, cheesy grins. "There. Jeanne and the Lucky Suit. By the way, have I mentioned that my granddaughter is single?"

This is not the first time she's mentioned her granddaughter. "Is that so?"

"That is indeed so." She shows me a photo of a lovely brunette with the cutest glasses and a spray of freckles all over her cheeks. Her hand is wrapped around a telescope.

"She is one smart lady, never met a question she won't ask, loves to stargaze, and, wouldn't you know, she just got into online dating."

I shudder. "I will never ever do online dating."

"Really?"

I raise my right hand. "Swear to God. You

don't know what you're getting into, or if they're who they say they are. And it's missing that certain *je ne sais quoi* of meeting someone in person and knowing if you have an actual connection and chemistry."

"That's a shame."

"Why is that a shame?"

She frowns. "Just think about all the women you're missing out on. All the chances you're not taking."

"Chances to have a date blow up in my face."

"Now that's not true. For instance, did you know that fifty-five percent of women say they only date men they meet online? They worry about the type of men they meet in person. The days of meeting people at bars is well over."

"Where's that stat from?"

She stares at the clear blue sky, tapping her chin. "I think I saw it in some *Psychology Today* survey. It got me to thinking—if you don't try online dating, it's sort of like playing poker without the suit of diamonds. Think about all the hands you'd miss out on."

Soon enough the auction begins, Jeanne snags the Camaro, and I leave wondering if there's a winning hand I've yet to encounter.

Later that night, I get online.

3

Kristen

I'm a glass-half-full person. And with my glass of iced tea, I'm eager to see what awaits me online.

Tablet tucked under my arm, cool tumbler in hand, I head to my deck and park myself next to my favorite thing—my trusty telescope.

"Hi, Nicolaus." I named the scope after one of my favorite scientists. After all, Nicolaus Copernicus did discover that Earth revolved around the sun, which is kind of a big deal.

I set down the tablet and glass, thread my fingers together, and crack my knuckles. I tap on the screen. "All right, algorithms of love. Who do you have for me tonight?"

A warm breeze blows by as I click open my dating profile.

"Whoa, Nelly."

That is one full inbox.

"Maybe I'm a babe and don't know it," I mutter, then laugh.

Please, if I were a babe, I'd be well aware. I'm simply the friendly neighborhood math whiz, the girl the boys asked to be their math tutor, their science tutor, and their applied calculus tutor.

As if applied calculus is hard.

Please.

But I suppose it can be if you don't spend all day mired in the gorgeousness of math problems.

That's what dating is. One giant math variable waiting to be solved. All I have to do is figure out the way to that connection and closeness I crave. I'll crack the code to a relationship. I know I will.

I click through the chat with Porter, but as he tells me about a new article on astrophysics, I keep picturing him with ladies' panties.

I switch over to Wallace, but as we opine on spreadsheets, I wonder if he has an ax somewhere in his house.

"Shake it off, shake it off."

Maybe I need an entirely new man to chat with. Someone Grams doesn't know about yet. Someone whose image she hasn't sullied in my head.

I return to the inbox and murmur appreciatively when I spot a new name, alongside a handsome picture of a thirty-something man with a fantastic smile, blond hair, bright blue eyes, and a face that, quite simply, looks kind.

ThinkingMan is his name. I laugh then scan his profile. His mantra is *"Opposites attract" is for magnets only*. Oh yes, it is, ThinkingMan.

I click open his note.

Dear Telescoper,

As you may have surmised, I'm not a big believer in the "opposites attract" theory. But I do love theories, and from your profile, I can see you do too. While I won't pretend to be someone I'm not, and I can't claim to be conversant in all things mathematical, I do love theories, debating them, dissecting them, and deconstructing them.

Also, stargazing rules. Did you know that the Andromeda Galaxy is going to crash into the Milky Way in 4.5 billion years? Of course you do. But what do you think that collision will look like?

Best,

ThinkingMan

That's literally one of my favorite things to discuss. With a crazy grin, I reply in the chat box.

Telescoper: Greetings, ThinkingMan! I don't

believe opposites attract either. In fact, there was a University of Kansas study that debunked the entire theory as it applies to relationships.

ThinkingMan: I do enjoy a good debunking. Especially since true similarities play the biggest part in pairings.

Telescoper: They do! Also, I like to think that collision will look like two stars ramming into each other, monster truck–style. But I suspect it'll be more like a river merging into an ocean.

ThinkingMan: I like that analogy. I can see that perfectly. One massive, bright, and beautiful galaxy flowing into another. I do think it'll be quite loud.

Telescoper: We're talking cover-your-eardrums loud.

ThinkingMan: Louder than the big bang?

Telescoper: I'd bet on it. By the way, did you know the Andromeda Galaxy is visible to the naked eye tonight?

ThinkingMan: I'm looking at it right now. It's always lovely on a moonless night.

Telescoper: I'm looking at Orion Nebula
right now.

ThinkingMan: Don't even tell me you have
some top-of-the-line NASA-style telescope. I'll be
too jealous.

Telescoper: I'd hate to make you jealous, then,
especially since it is an awfully big scope.

ThinkingMan: Oh no, you didn't just go there!

Telescoper: Oh yes, I did! It is huge though.
After all, what I don't spend on shoes and cosmos,
I spend on my telescope.

ThinkingMan: So you gave up cosmos for the
cosmos.

Telescoper: Nice wordplay. Ten points to you.

ThinkingMan: And for ten points, I'll go check
out the Orion Nebula too.

As we chat about the constellation and how it
looks this evening, and I gaze at the night sky, I
don't have to wonder if he's looking at the same
stars. He *is*.

And even though it's premature to think this

means anything, I'm giving my first swing at online dating a gold star.

I'll admit it.

I'm eager to talk to ThinkingMan again the next evening after I come home from work.

He's not online though, so I put aside my disappointment, burying myself in a presentation on new ways to harness wind power to make dishwashers run more efficiently.

Midway through, Grams knocks on my door, dressed in her mechanic coveralls. "I need to do some work on my Camaro. Can you babysit my Crock-Pot?"

"Isn't that the point of a Crock-Pot? It babysits itself?"

"It does, true. But dinner should be ready in a few minutes, and I want you to turn it off."

I grab my tablet and head to her place next door. When I reach the kitchen, she hands me her phone. "Take this too."

"Your phone also needs babysitting?"

She shoots me a *duh* look. "Of course it does. I'm in the middle of a game. I'm close to hitting a poker streak, but I need to get some work done on this car for Betty. Can you take over my game?"

"Sure. Do you want me to crush your opponent or just whup her butt gently like you usually do?"

She laughs. "A gentle whupping will suffice. But it's not a *she* I'm playing with."

I furrow my brow. "Who am I crushing on your behalf, then?"

"My new poker buddy. I met him at the car auction, and he's quite friendly."

"You're flirting with a poker friend?"

"Did I say I was flirting?"

"Knowing you, you're probably flirting. You said the view was nice."

"I meant the view of the cars! The junkyard was full of gorgeous, lovely cars calling out to me."

"Ah, so you were perving on the cars. Got it." I tap my temple like I'm filing away this piece of intel.

"Just. Play. The. Hands."

"What if he wants to chat?"

"Chat with him," she says breezily.

I arch a brow, adopt a spooky tone. "What if he's an ax murderer though?"

"He's not, because I met him in person."

"Question: do you think ax murderers wear name tags that identify them by profession?"

"I think you are as inquisitive today as you were when you were thirteen and I took you to the zoo and you had a gazillion questions. And do you know what I encouraged you to do then?"

I smile. "Talk to the zookeeper and ask all of them."

"Yes, so feel free to screen this man to your heart's content."

"I will definitely handle your man-friend." I wink.

She heads down to the garage, and I open her poker game, perusing the status. I see a chat window open, and I decide this is my chance to vet Grams's new guy. To find out if he's good enough for her. Just call me Inspector Kristen.

All right, LuckySuit, let's see what you've got.

4

Cameron

A pocket-size monkey swings from a tree branch.

I snap a photo of the primate then several more as he somersaults to another branch inside Monkey Jungle.

Lulu points at my subject. "You're going to tell me you want monkey-shaped chocolate next."

"Sounds brilliant. Seems my photographic pursuits are good for our business. Maybe I should work on poker chips and slot machine pictures for good luck since Las Vegas is next on the itinerary."

"And I have all the faith in the world you'll nab more deals there, and soon Lulu's Chocolates will be carried in the swankiest hotels on the Strip."

"From your mouth to the dotted-line's ears," I say as we wander through the wildlife park teeming with monkeys of all shapes and sizes.

When Lulu discovered the existence of a place called Monkey Jungle near our meeting location, she begged me to take her here once business was done.

She squeezes my shoulder. "And holy smokes, did we kick butt today or what?" She high-fives me for probably the tenth time since our pitch meeting with the hotel. They loved her and her energy, but especially her chocolate. And they love the deal I'm putting together for them.

We amble over to the swimming hole, chatting as I capture a series of shots of a monkey bathing. "What a little exhibitionist."

"I don't know. He looks kind of shy. Maybe it's his first public bath," Lulu suggests.

I linger on that word.

First.

I've no plans to take a public bath, but as we walk, I keep mulling over a little thing I never thought I'd do—online dating.

It's not my style.

Not one bit.

I believe in the personal zip and zing. I believe in looking in someone's eyes. I believe in instinct. Heck, that's how Jeanne and Joe met, and they seem to have hit it off and, I suspect, will be dating any day.

I've been single long enough, and while I don't need to put a ring on anyone today or tomorrow, I'd rather get down on one knee sooner rather than later. I'd like to find the right person. The person I want to spend my time with.

"Hey, what do you think of online dating?"

Lulu squeals, grabbing my shoulders as a monkey with a raccoon mask stares at us. "Are you trying it?"

"I might be . . ."

She pounces all over my answer. "Seriously? Are you? Can I help you set up your profile?"

"Maybe I already set it up," I tease her.

"Can I see it?" She sounds like she's about to bounce off the trees.

"Wouldn't you like to see it?"

"Yes, I would. That's why I'm asking you. I want you to find your soul mate."

"And you think my soul mate is online? Hanging out somewhere on the interwebs, chilling and waiting for her man to upload his profile?"

"Yes. And when you find her, you'll know it."

"How will I know it?"

"You won't be able to stop talking to each other. You'll chat about all the things that keep you awake at night. You'll talk until the wee hours of the morning."

"Is that how things are with you and Leo these days?"

Lulu brings her finger to her lips. "Shh."

"Why are you shushing me? Leo's in New York. He can't hear you."

"I know that, but I don't want to jinx it. I'm still trying to figure it all out."

"I don't believe in jinxes."

"What do you believe in?"

"I believe in chemistry and chance when it comes to matters of the heart."

A little later, I take her to the airport and send her back to New York, letting her know I'll see her again in Manhattan. As I head to my car, I do some quick photoshopping on my phone then send her a picture of the gawking monkey now perched on her shoulder.

She replies with a string of monkey emoticons.

I return to my hotel. Since it's June and high eighties even in the evening, I head to the pool area, grab a lounge chair, and enjoy a little sunset breeze and people-watching. A woman in a silver bikini rides a unicycle, followed by an Elvis imper- sonator on stilts. A sign hangs from his neck —*Photos free, Hugs $5.*

I snap a free photo.

As the sun dips lower on the horizon, I turn to the poker app, thinking about online dating as I consider how many cards to hold and how many to fold. They're all stinkers, so I draw mostly fresh cards.

Can online dating truly lead to a soul mate? Call me skeptical. But curious too.

As I study the new cards—they aren't any better—a chat window pops up.

HotRodLover: I'm doubtful you can win a single hand.

Whoa. Jeanne is going all in on the trash talk. That's not usually her style, but I can play this way. I crack my knuckles.

LuckySuit: Is that so? Me beating you repeatedly isn't enough?

HotRodLover: Tonight, prepare to be vanquished.

I blink and scrub a hand across my jaw. What has gotten into Jeanne? She's so feisty today.

LuckySuit: Try me. Just try me.

HotRodLover: I will. There you go.

She plays her hand, winning easily. I regroup, order a beer from the poolside waiter, and we play a few more rounds. She demolishes me.

LuckySuit: Fine, fine. You're on fire tonight. I'm man enough to admit you brought your A game.

HotRodLover: Don't I always?

LuckySuit: That you do . . .

HotRodLover: Speaking of A games, what would you say is the most important thing on the path to happiness?

I crack up. I swear, this woman is a hoot.

LuckySuit: You're awfully philosophical all of a sudden. You don't want to segue into a new conversation topic? You just go for it?

HotRodLover: Please. Who needs segues? Plus, I like philosophy. And happiness. And contemplation. So fess up.

LuckySuit: I suppose I'd have to say kindness, fine chocolate, friends, family, giving back, good wine and great beer, and exotic travel.

HotRodLover: Ooh la la. You're fancy-pants in a lucky suit.

LuckySuit: I'm not all about the jet-setting life-style! I did mention family, friends, giving back.

HotRodLover: I'm all for those things too, except wine, just for the record. Now, tell me what family means to you . . .

I laugh at her question. It's like I'm being quizzed all of a sudden. I take a gulp of the beer.

LuckySuit: Wait a second. It's my turn. What are your happiness must-haves?

HotRodLover: You can't ask the same question!

LuckySuit: Why not?

HotRodLover: Rules.

LuckySuit: Rules? What rules?

HotRodLover: The rules of conversation say you must ask a new question.

As a woman in a black bikini dives into the pool, I look up, thinking of new questions and briefly wondering why my car auction and card-playing friend is so sparky tonight. A possibility tugs on my brain like a fish on a lure. I'm not sure if I'm right, but I've got a feeling, so I play out the line to see what bites.

LuckySuit: Do you believe in luck, chance, or fate?

HotRodLover: I believe fate is the creation of nonscientists. I believe luck is random happenstance and chance is simply a variable we scientists have to account for.

And that's another clue. Right there, dropped like a delicious bread crumb. I pick it up.

LuckySuit: "We" scientists?

HotRodLover: I mean "we" as in the royal "we."

LuckySuit: Now you're royal?

HotRodLover: Royally going to beat you in the next hand.

And she does just that. Then she kills me again. Each time, she's sassy. She's witty. She's firing off all sorts of one-liners, and it sure seems like my fishing line is catching something.

HotRodLover: Are you ready to admit defeat at my hand?

LuckySuit: Never surrender. I'll soldier on.

HotRodLover: Ah, I see you are relentless. Would you describe yourself as relentless?

That's an easy question to answer. All I have to do is look at the elbow grease Lulu and I put into building the concept of the stores and her line of chocolate. *Yes.*

But before I reply, I set the phone down on the wooden table next to my lounge chair. I stare up at the darkening sky, twilight falling at last. The stars will shove their way to the blanket of night soon enough.

Reminding me of something.

Something that explains why I'm liking chatting with Jeanne in a way I shouldn't be liking. Something that tells me that maybe Jeanne isn't Jeanne.

She said: "*We* scientists."

She loves to ask questions.

She's particularly fiery.

I believe I've caught something on the fishing line.

And I'm going to turn the tables on her.

LuckySuit: Absolutely. I am tenacious, determined, and focused. What about you? Oh, wait, am I allowed to ask the same questions? No, of course not. Let me rephrase. What is your favorite quality in yourself?

As the three dots flash on the screen, I can't wait to see what Not-Jeanne says.

5

_____

Kristen

The Crock-Pot is off.

The presentation is done.

I'm winning at poker.

Grams is still tinkering in the garage.

And I'm weirdly having a blast inspecting her new man-friend. He's hilarious. And forward. And direct.

I love a good question-asker. *What is my favorite quality?*

As I drum my unpolished nails against the counter, I laugh out loud. It's the very quality that has me talking to Grams's man-friend. And it's the quality I learned from the woman herself. So it's with complete forthrightness that I answer.

HotRodLover: Inquisitiveness.

But once I send that, it's not enough. So I add a little something more.

HotRodLover: As you can see, since I've demonstrated it tonight. I possess it in buckets.

LuckySuit: Indeed you have, and it seems you have amassed quite a bucketful. Can I assume that inquisitiveness extends to the heavens above us? The stars in all their glory?

Whoa. Grams's friend is reeling me in with his talk of my favorite thing. He's getting the full seal of approval.

HotRodLover: My curiosity extends to the far reaches of the Milky Way and beyond. After all, knowing the stars helps us to know ourselves, I like to say.

LuckySuit: And why do you like to say that?

HotRodLover: They remind us of our place in

the universe—how vast the universe truly is, but how we can still play valuable roles in it.

LuckySuit: Ah, is there anything better than philosophizing on why we're here?

HotRodLover: Nothing, nothing at all!

My face glows. He's so not a serial killer. He's perfect for me.

I mean for her.

He's perfect for her.

He's absolutely ideal for Grams. I start to tap a reply, when my own phone dings. I ignore it at first, but it chimes again, and I check it.

Mom: Hey, has Grams said anything to you about the guy she met at the car auction?

I squint at her question like it holds some clue to who the guy on the other end of the poker chat really is. I play coy to see what else Mom knows.

Kristen: No. What guy? Did she tell you anything about him?

Mom: Not enough! I'm trying to figure out if she's gone on a date with him yet. She mentioned to me that they'd chatted after she snagged the Camaro, and I was hoping it would lead to something more. :)

Kristen: Well, did you ask her?

Mom: Gee. Why didn't I think of that? ;)

Kristen: Want me to play spy for you?

Mom: Yes, go full 007.

Kristen: Anything for the woman who owns the high-rise building and lets her mom and me live here at cost.

Mom: Cost? Lady, I let you two live there at way less than cost.

Kristen: The things we do for family.

As I hit send, I spot a reply from the dating site, and a new sensation blooms inside me. *Hope.*

Hope that ThinkingMan has reached back out, because chatting with LuckySuit reminds me how much I liked talking to ThinkingMan. And that's exactly why I started a profile in the first place—to find that connection.

I click over, and there he is.

ThinkingMan: Hey, Telescoper. Are you looking at the stars again tonight? I hear Cassiopeia is going to show off and twinkle.

Telescoper: She always struts her stuff! But right now? I'm chatting. And thinking.

ThinkingMan: They are two of my favorite activities.

Telescoper: I'd like to ask what the third is, but that might be too forward. So let me ask something else—why don't you believe opposites attract?

ThinkingMan: It's a myth. A fairy tale. It's handed down from storytellers because it makes a good story.

As I type, Grams's man replies on *her* phone, and I whip my head to that screen, setting my phone down before I can write back to ThinkingMan.

I read LuckySuit's answer, trying to remember what we were last talking about in the poker app.

Like a juggler, I'm tossing the conversation balls higher in the air, trying to keep my eyes on all of them. First ball—Mom and I were discussing some guy Grams met at the auction. Second ball —ThinkingMan and I are chatting about stars and opposites repelling. Third ball—Grams's friend LuckySuit and I were gabbing about . . .

We were talking about understanding how we all fit into the bigger picture. That's what his reply is about.

LuckySuit: I had a feeling you liked all things logical, scientific, and mathematical.

HotRodLover: Math is the bomb. I could do it all night and never grow tired.

LuckySuit: All night long? That's some serious numerical stamina.

I shimmy my shoulders back and forth. It's like I've consumed ten energy drinks and I'm tossing the balls in a dazzlingly high arc. I am a most excellent spy.

HotRodLover: I once entered a multiplication marathon. I won.

LuckySuit: Impressive. How long did it last?

HotRodLover: Why, I thought you'd never ask. ;) Seven hours and ten minutes. I won a calculator. Have you ever done a marathon?

LuckySuit: Yes. Do you want to ask how long it was?

HotRodLover: As a matter of fact, I think I do want to ask that. :)

I reread my last reply. And the one before. And before.

My jaw drops.

I'm falling too far out of character. I don't sound like Grams. I sound like *me* talking. Admittedly, Grams's guy is kind of cool and interesting, and he's passing all my screening tests. But I need to make sure I don't sound too much like her twenty-eight-year-old granddaughter.

Or like I'm flirting with him.

Wait. Am I flirting with this guy? Maybe a little?

It's kind of weird that I'm enjoying it.

I take a breath.

I'll just go chat with ThinkingMan for a bit, so I don't get too carried away with the charade again.

I toggle over to exit the poker app when LuckySuit replies, and my eyes pop wide.

LuckySuit: And might that be because you're actually Kristen?

Busted. The balls tumble down.

6

Cameron

Someone turns up the speakers, and Panic! at the Disco takes over the evening air poolside.

Smiling to myself, I reread the conversation. I had a feeling, and I was right.

And I have to admit, I think Jeanne might have been onto something when she dropped her anvil-size hints yesterday at the car auction about her granddaughter being single. She clearly thought we'd be a good match, and maybe she had the right idea.

Kristen is one fiery lady, and I dig that.

I dig that a hell of a lot.

But I especially like honesty.

And Kristen's showing it right now when she answers my question.

HotRodLover: Gulp.

LuckySuit: Would that be a yes?

HotRodLover: I think it's patently obvious the answer is a yes. As in yes, I'm Kristen. I'm the scientist. I'm her twenty-eight-year-old grand-daughter. I'm weirdly good at poker. I also did a multiplication marathon post-college, so you can call me a geek girl, but I'll have you know I competed in Roller Derby in high school and college, so yeah, they balance each other. At least, that's what I tell myself.

LuckySuit: Let's talk about this Roller Derby. That's seriously impressive.

HotRodLover: Hold on. We *can't* keep talking. I can't talk to you like this. I was simply trying to ascertain what your intentions were with my grams!

I spit up my drink. Seriously? I stare at the question on the screen. She seriously just asked me that? I crack up as I type.

LuckySuit: My intentions with Jeanne? That's

why you were working me over like a detective trying to shake down a perp?

HotRodLover: That's exactly the effect I was going for. I see it worked.

I swear I can picture the bespectacled brunette perfectly—hands on hips, arms akimbo, chin up. Challenging me. And yes, for the record, she looks cute in the photo my mind just snapped. I don't need Photoshop for her.

LuckySuit: Let me get this straight. You were slinging your litany of questions at me to determine if I'd be a good man to date your grandma?

HotRodLover: Of course. Someone has to look out for her. Family is important, like we were saying.

LuckySuit: Family is mega, super-duper, supremely important.

HotRodLover: So . . . ticktock. Intentions. What are they, mister?

She is too adorable. Too in your face. Too bold. And I like it.

LuckySuit: Let me lay things out for you. I have no intentions with her other than friendship. And there are many reasons for that. But one of them starts and ends with family—my uncle is interested in her! Which also means . . . wait for it . . . I'm not your Grams's age.

She doesn't reply right away, and as the indicator lights bounce around, I snap a photo of the darkening sky then take in my surroundings, enjoying how different Miami is from my current home in Manhattan.

I breathe in the salt air and the warm breeze. I hear someone splashing, and I wish momentarily that this life was mine. I take the time to savor everything that's not New York City, from the pace, to the pools, to the waves, to the vast stretches of sand.

Most of all, to the mood. I do love the vibe of this tropical city. Especially now.

HotRodLover: So your uncle is the guy from the car auction?

LuckySuit: He runs it.

HotRodLover: He's not an ax murderer?

LuckySuit: Not that I'm aware of.

HotRodLover: Because you'd know if he was? He'd tell you?

LuckySuit: We're close. I'd like to think he'd divulge his profession as well as his hobbies.

HotRodLover: How do you think that sort of thing comes up? "By the way, last night I accomplished a career high of six bloody murders."

LuckySuit: Ah, so he's not just an ax murderer but a successful one? Also, it's adorable that you're screening her beaux. I suppose on behalf of Uncle Joe I should inquire if Jeanne's into him.

HotRodLover: Not to be direct, but also to be totally direct, who are you? I thought you were some man-friend of hers, and it turns out you are indeed her man-friend, but you're also not her age. You're younger. Please say you're not a teenager!

LuckySuit: I've been out of my teens for a while, but my AARP membership is still a ways off.

HotRodLover: Fine. The other question. Who exactly are you?

I glance at my shirt, my shorts, my drink. I consider the photos I take. I think about the eclectic mix of rock and indie music on my phone. I imagine my friends in New York. Who am I? I'm a lot of things.

LuckySuit: I'm the guy who believes in luck and chance. I'm the dude who plays online poker with your grandma because she's a riot and she makes me laugh, and she has ever since I met her at the car auction the other month. I'm the person who likes music and books and philosophy. I think chocolate is heaven on earth, and beer is a damn delicious beverage. And I like people. Always have. It's possible the word "gregarious" has been used to describe me. That's probably why I get along well with Jeanne. I'm outgoing, and so is she. She's also proud of you.

HotRodLover: That's quite a résumé you shared. Almost like an online dating profile. By the way, what has she said about me? Maybe that I'm an inquisitive troublemaker?

LuckySuit: Oh, I figured that out on my own. :)

As for Jeanne, she brags about you, but she never mentioned Roller Derby, and now I'm dying to know all the details. Color me intrigued. What was your derby name?

HotRodLover: Calcu Lass.

LuckySuit: Was Zero Sum Dame not available? Wait. Don't answer. Calcu Lass is officially the best name ever.

HotRodLover: Why, thank you. I sure did rock a pair of high socks and skates. But enough about me. Who are you? What's your name?

LuckySuit: I'm Cameron. And in case she hasn't told you, I'm from New York, I'm in the chocolate business, and I have my sights set on a Ferrari, but I've yet to pull the trigger.

HotRodLover: I'm in the market for a Bugatti, for what it's worth.

HotRodLover: Also, gotta go.

She logs out of the app.

7

Kristen

The front door slams shut, and I sit up straight, my breath coming quickly.

Shoot. I don't want Grams to read what we were saying in her app. I will never hear the end of it if she knows how badly I flirted with her friend.

Or how *well*, I should say.

Because that was some seriously good flirting, and am I ever glad he's not *her* prospective man.

"The red beauty is nearly ready for Betty," Grams says, exhaling with relief, her work boots clomping across the floor.

My shoulders tighten, and my thumbs fly across the keyboard. "That's good." I scroll up, delete the conversation with LuckySuit, and sign out of the app. Then I grab my phone and exit the dating app, right as Grams turns the corner into the kitchen.

She's smiling.

I'm smiling too.

Wait. I need to wipe this smile off my face. I can't let on how much I enjoyed chatting with Cameron.

Or can I?

"Did you crush my friend?" she asks as she heads to the sink to wash her hands.

"I did."

"So it was an excellent night of poker and perhaps conversation?"

"We chatted a bit." The words come out stiffly.

"And?"

I'm still not sure what their connection is, so I backpedal. "I grilled him. To make sure he's good enough for you. I don't want him to stalk you or grandma-nap you."

She slaps her thigh and bursts into laughter. "He's thirty-two. He's *your* age. Not mine."

Even though he told me he wasn't too much older or too much younger, I'm glad to have the confirmation. "Oh, thank God."

"Why do you say that?" She pounces, and I suppose there's no point being coy.

I admit the truth. "Because he's quite fun and interesting and clever."

She beams, a smile that stretches to Neptune and back. "Cameron sure is, isn't he? And quite a looker, I might add."

"Really?" My voice rises. I try to erase the stupid bit of hope in it. I shouldn't be happy he's good-looking, but holy hell, I am. I almost want to ask for a photo, but that'd be gauche.

But then I remember something he said.

And I deflate.

There's no point in a photo. He lives in New York.

"He's in town for a few more days," she adds, and my heart balloons back up.

But still, with all my willpower, I resist asking to see him. He's leaving, so it's pointless. "That's great. I'm seriously behind. I need to go."

I grab my tablet and phone and skedaddle out of her place. But being next door is too close, too claustrophobic, and there are too many online men occupying too much real estate in my brain.

I text my best friend, Piper, and ask if she can finagle a late-night meeting.

* * *

By the fifth hole, I've caught Piper up on all my online dating escapades.

"This is fabulous news," Piper declares as she swings her golf club. She's a whiz at miniature golf, and I wish I could become one by osmosis.

"And why is this such a fabulous development?" I position my purple golf ball on the tee, the bright lights illuminating the course even at this late hour.

"So many of my clients these days are meeting online." Piper is something of a wedding planner, so she knows the intricacies of how couples meet and bind in holy matrimony. "Many of the online matches get engaged and married sooner, and often they seem to get along better. That's what those of us in the wedding biz call a hole in one."

I look up from the ball, club in hand. "What percentage of your clients have met online?"

She screws up the corner of her lips and glances toward the sky. Piper lives in New York, but she's in town prepping for a wedding she's working on. "Well, since you are sort of obsessed with numbers and statistics, I'll say seventy-six percent. But it's also entirely possible I might have pulled that number out of thin air."

"Well, why don't you pull it out of un-thin air? Why don't you tell me how many people really meet online?"

She pats my shoulder then gestures to the tee. "Take your turn first."

I whack the ball, watching as it rolls underneath a swinging pirate ship, landing miserably far from the hole. "You're trying to get me to mess up."

"You do an excellent job of that on your own, which is why I love playing with you."

"Someday you'll meet someone who's amazing at mini golf, and it will be unbearably difficult for you to actually have to compete," I tease.

"But that day hasn't come yet."

We walk along the green to the balls and Piper taps hers lightly, sending it to the hole, then answers my question. "Easily more than half of the weddings I do are for couples who met online. It's the most popular way people meet these days."

I hit the purple ball, and it mocks me by zipping close to the hole then doglegging away. Evil orb. "My grams thinks online dating will lead me to Jack the Ripper's door."

"Maybe it'll lead to Jack Rip-off-your-clothes-and-bang-you-against-a-door."

I wiggle my eyebrows. "A girl can dream."

With the club in her hand, she presses her palms together. "A girl can pray."

For a second, I wonder if LuckySuit is a bang-you-against-the-door kind of guy. Then I wonder where that thought came from.

Oh yeah, chatting with him.

With the guy who lives in New York, so it's pointless.

Piper flicks her chestnut hair off her shoulder. "So, tell me about these guys that you've been meeting online. I'm dying to hear."

As I tap, tap, tap to five strokes on a par two, I tell her about LuckySuit and what went down tonight. "His real name is Cameron."

"What's his last name, so we can online stalk him and see if he's Hemsworthy."

My shoulders sag. "I didn't get it."

"Ask your grams."

I shake my head. "I can't."

"Why?"

"It'd be like admitting she was right."

"Oh, well, you can't do that."

"But there's this other guy . . ."

Her eyes pop wide in avid interest, and I update her on my conversation with ThinkingMan.

"When are you going to meet him?" she asks as we stroll to the next hole.

The possibility makes my skin spark with both nerves and excitement. "Should I meet him?"

"You should meet him *and* you should meet Cameron."

"But Cameron doesn't even live here."

She shrugs happily. "It can't hurt. Just tell your grams you want to meet her friend. It's not admitting defeat. It's opening yourself up to possibility."

Funny, how earlier I was juggling one possibility. Now there are two. And both are appealing.

Especially when I find a message from one the next morning.

8

Cameron

My phone rings while I'm jogging along the beach as the pink light of dawn stretches across the sky.

"Hey, Jeanne," I say. "What's shaking?"

"Not the earth, thank heavens."

"Indeed, that's a good thing. By the way, did you hear about last night? And how I chatted with your granddaughter?"

"Only a little. Seems my Kristen deleted the conversation the two of you had, but I'm not a spy. I'm simply a little old lady who wants her granddaughter to have a nice date with a nice man."

I slow my pace, a little surprised she went for it. But then, I shouldn't be, given how she mentioned her at the auction. "You know you're not a little old lady. You're a wise, clever woman, and I bet you have some plan for me."

I can hear her smile. "You figured me out. Let's cut to the chase. She liked you. I think you liked her. Would you like to meet her today at four p.m.? She has a shortened workday."

She names a popular spot in the Wynwood neighborhood.

I stop in my tracks, and before I can think too deeply on all the reasons to say no, I say yes.

9

Kristen

Before I leave for work, a message blinks at me.

My stomach flip-flops when I see the name.

My mind is a swirl of possibilities, switching back and forth between two men—LuckySuit and ThinkingMan.

But only one of them is asking me out.

ThinkingMan: Would you want to meet today at four p.m.?

I say yes, and I hope it doesn't come out breathlessly online. Then I ask for his name.

ThinkingMan: Mac.

Telescoper: I'm Kristen.

ThinkingMan: See you this afternoon.

I can't wait.

10

Cameron

"Look at you. All decked out for a blind date." Joe whistles at me as we chat in the lobby bar. "And you finally look like you belong here."

I arch a brow. "I beg to differ. There is not a white jacket or an ounce of pink or pastel on me." I gesture to my outfit—jeans and a navy-blue polo. Simple, casual. Fitting for a blind date.

At least, I think so. I haven't been on one since my first year out of college when my friend Mariana set me up with a preschool teacher who, it turned out, liked to snort glue.

I'll just say I'm glad I don't have kids in her school.

And Mariana is too.

Joe waves a hand dismissively. "Just kidding.

You're so New York in your clothes, you're a lost cause."

"And you practically match the art deco theme here," I say, since the man looks like he can only exist in the tropics—he's gone all in on the pink shirt, for crying out loud. Yet, he's a stylish dude.

We talk some more, and I finish off my iced tea and check my watch. "I need to jet. But what about you? Are you going to get some cojones and finally let Jeanne know you've got it bad for her? I saw the way the two of you were making googly eyes at each other at the auction the other day."

"Maybe I already have . . ."

"You sly dog. Such a fast worker." I toss a twenty on the sleek silver counter of the bar. "Wait. Are you pulling my leg again?"

"Maybe I already asked her to marry me."

I clap his shoulder. "I can see I'm getting no straight answers from you."

"Have fun on your date, young turk. I'll have fun on mine with Jeanne."

I grin. "Excellent. And soon I'll be saying have fun on your honeymoon, Silver Fox."

He raises his glass in a toast. "You never know. I do have it bad for her."

"You never do know," I echo, and I take off to meet Kristen.

* * *

A happy blue alien tries to devour a yellow flower.

Next to the peppy creature, a green bug chases a pink caterpillar.

I snap photo after photo of the street art, capturing the graffiti on the walls in the Wynwood neighborhood, a mecca for outdoor art with more than forty murals. I arrived early, since it's always better to be early.

Plus, taking pictures gives me something to do as I wait. Keeps me busy. That way I don't have to focus on nerves.

Wait.

I don't feel any.

Of course I don't feel any.

Why would I? Just because I haven't been on a blind date since the glue-snorter.

I snap another shot, telling myself it'll be fine, it'll be good, and the date will simply pass the time. Nothing more can come of it, so I'll just have fun. That's all it can ever be.

"I see we both like to peer through lenses."

I lower my camera when I hear the pretty voice, turning around to see a woman in red glasses, those jeans that end at the calves, and a silky light-blue tank top. She's prettier than any blind date has ever been in the history of the universe, with chestnut locks that curl in waves over her shoulders, freckles, and a nose that's nothing short of adorable.

Hell, I stand no chance of *not* liking her. "Telescopes for you, I presume, with all your stargazing?"

For a second, her brow knits, as if I've said something odd. "Yes, I'm the Telescoper."

The designation makes me smile, so I point to myself. "The Camera-er."

She laughs. "Each gives a different perspective on the world."

"I'm a big fan of different perspectives," I add, enjoying the view of her so very much, and the conversational potential seems promising too.

"Ditto." She licks her lips, tucks a strand of hair over her ear.

I extend a hand. "I presume you're Kristen?"

She laughs lightly, like maybe she's a touch nervous too. "Last time I checked I was." She takes my hand, and we shake. "Good to meet you, Mac."

I furrow my brow. Did she just call me Mac? But the woman is nervous, and I don't need to correct her this second. I'll remind her of my name when she's not so nervous. I gesture to the blue alien overlord. "Glad we could do this. I've been wanting to check out these murals. Did you see the one with Yoda painted every color of the rainbow?"

Her green eyes widen. They twinkle with specks of gold. "No, but I think we should see what kind of points we deserve for creative selfies. Since, you know, we gave out points for wordplay."

I rack my brain a moment, trying to remember when we assigned points for wordplay. I don't recall, but it sounds like something we'd have done, so I go with it. "Most creative selfie wins . . ." I stroke my chin as we walk. "Hmm. What's a good prize?"

She snaps her fingers. "I know. Whoever wins gets to ask five questions in a row."

"You and your questions," I say, laughing,

She shoots me a quizzical look, as if I've thrown her off.

But maybe we're both still in the nervous zone. Best to act like a comedian does when he or she is terrified of the crowd—never let them see you sweat.

I segue into another topic, hoping it eases any remaining awkwardness. "Tell me more about your interest in astronomy. Were you one of those kids who got a telescope for Christmas and it ignited a lifelong love?"

"Exactly! It was like Santa knew my true soul."

"He is one smart dude." I wink. "Sounds like your parents knew you well."

"They did." She taps her chin as we wander past a geometric painting of pink-and-blue prisms. "Actually, if memory serves, *they* gave me my first scope. They didn't want Santa getting credit for something so good."

"Now those are some seriously smart parents. What did Santa get you that year? Socks?"

"Coal," she deadpans.

"I see you've spent some time on the naughty list."

Her eyes twinkle with mischief. "Sometimes I still wind up on it."

And I'm officially a goner. This woman—I like her. I like her a hell of a lot already. This is what I'm talking about—chemistry, zip, zing. It's all about the in-person connection.

"What do you know? I've found myself on top of that list a few times." I flash her a smile, and when she grins back, I'm done for. Her smile is magical and sexy at the same time—gleaming white teeth and glossy lips that beg to be kissed.

She nudges my arm. "I can't believe you've been keeping your naughty adventures from me."

"Well, I had to save something to discuss on our date."

She laughs again. "Fess up. How did you end up on the naughty list when you were a kid?"

"Ah, you want the kid-naughty list stuff?"

"We can save the adult-naughty list conversation for a second date," she stage-whispers.

I tap my temple, as if I'm filing that away then making a note to myself. "Makes plans for second date." I sigh happily. "Okay, kid stuff. Let's see. When I was ten, I told my sister her birthday was wrong. I made her a fake birth certificate in Photoshop. I was always into taking pictures and doing cool things with them. Or cruel things. So I showed it to her, and for a few days, she believed she was a year older and kept asking why she was held back in school."

Her jaw goes slack, and her eyes widen. "You were masterfully naughty."

"That's nothing compared to her revenge."

"What did she do?"

"She knew my sweet tooth was off the charts. So she made me a pie spiked with hot sauce. Brownies with salt instead of sugar. But that's not the worst of it: she then made a batch of real chocolate cookies and put raisins in them." I pretend to sniffle and then rub fake tears off my face. "That was the worst."

Kristen's nose crinkles. "She wins the prank wars. That is fantastic." We turn the corner. "My grandma and I like to prank each other. One time she set the autocorrect options on my phone to *eggplant*, *Uranus*, and *dik-dik*, which is actually a tiny antelope."

I chuckle. "That does not surprise me in the least. She's a character. Also, tiny antelopes are adorable."

She stops in front of a giant pink mushroom. "I've told you about her?"

I narrow my eyes. Is she crazy? Then I remind myself—never let them see you sweat. And never let on you know she's sweating. "Of course you did. And nothing about her surprises me."

She shakes her head, as if she's shaking off a thought. She points to the end of the block. "Anyway, there's Yoda. Let's see how we do."

I pretend to put my arm around the green dude and snap a selfie, and then Kristen puckers up like she's going to kiss him, capturing that on her phone. We compare, and I concede. "Why am I not surprised? You definitely win. You kissing Yoda earns all the points."

She pumps a fist. "Yes, Twenty Questions time."

I hold up five fingers. "You get five questions."

She pretends to roll up her sleeves. "All right. Are you ready?"

"Hit me. I'm already warmed up from your barrage of questions last night."

She arches a brow. "I didn't think it was a barrage."

I laugh. "What exactly would you call it?"

"I didn't think I asked that many."

"That many? It was a firing squad of questions." I soften my tone as we near a mural of a flamingo. "But I didn't mind. I enjoyed them all. I was thoroughly, completely entertained to the max."

She smiles. "Me too. Our conversations have been fun."

But it does feel like we've had them separately, and I'm not sure why.

11

Kristen

I can't quite put my finger on it.

It's almost as if he's not the guy I've been chatting with on the dating site.

But he looks exactly like his online photo, which is rare. Usually they're a few years off, give or take. This guy looks precisely like his shot, almost like his picture was snapped a few days ago. Plus, Mac is so handsome, it's almost unreal.

Still, it's as if we're in parallel worlds—close, but not quite running on the same track.

So even though I've earned my five questions, and even though I should make them meaningful, getting-to-know-you ones, like *What book would you read if stranded on a desert island?*, or ones that highlight a person's sense of humor, like *If you're clean when you get out of the shower, how does a towel become dirty?*, I opt for something simpler in the hope that I can figure out if we're connecting or disconnecting.

I gesture to the mural of the flamingo. "Wouldn't it be funny if the color of our hair was a result of our diet?" He gives me a look that says I'm borderline bonkers, so I explain. "Flamingos are pink because of the pigments in their food. Carotenoids. And they eat pink food—shrimp, algae, crustaceans . . ."

He points to the saucy birds ornamenting the side of a building. "That does sound familiar. I remember learning that at some point. Now, have you ever thought about this twist—what if they ate blue fish or green birds? Would they be a different color?"

"We'd probably have emerald-green flamingos all over our mugs, license plates, and other gift shop trinkets."

His fingers grip his skull then explode. "A whole different spectrum of tchotchkes."

"It's odd, isn't it? I'm pretty sure in this flamingo-carotenoid universe, I'd be green. I'm secretly addicted to kale."

He looks at his watch. "I'm going to have to leave right now."

"Why?" I laugh.

He crosses his arms. They're quite toned, I notice. His biceps look nice and strong and would feel great wrapped around me, I bet. A zing shoots down my chest as he shakes his head. "No one is secretly addicted to kale. So you're either an alien or a robot or a celebrity on a fad diet, and I can't date any of those."

I smile. I love that he keeps saying "date." It makes me feel like we're both enjoying this in equal amounts.

I lean toward *connecting*.

I hold up my hand like I'm taking an oath. "I do. I love it. I make no bones about it."

"No one loves kale. It takes like ten years to finish one leaf."

"You've never had my roasted kale with sunflower seeds," I say, as if I'm offering a seductive treat.

"While I do like the way you talk it up, I'm sure I will never eat it." He steps closer. "Feel free to offer something else though."

"Chocolate cookies with raisins?" I purr.

He laughs. Definitely *connecting*.

"Okay, what color would your hair be?" I ask, using this chance to check him out more. The evening sun glints off his dark-blond hair, highlighting strands of gold and showing off how soft it looks. I bet it'd feel great slipping through my fingers as I kissed him.

Oh hell. Do I ever I want to kiss him. I barely know him, but what I know I like enough to want to crush my lips to his and find out if our chemistry extends to kisses.

"Blue."

"Your hair would be blue?" I ask.

"Blueberries. That's a true addiction. They're delicious, juicy, pretty, and you can down a whole basket in seconds flat. Bonus—blueberries even taste good in chocolate."

We resume our walk past the graffiti art. "You'd look cute with blue hair."

"And you'd look cute with kale-colored hair," he says, as if he's choking on the words.

"It's okay. I know someday you'll be chowing down on roasted kale and eating your words."

He cracks up then clears his throat. "But honestly, my hair would probably be brown. I do love chocolate more than nearly anything."

I hum, mulling that over. LuckySuit said he loved chocolate too. But a lot of people like chocolate. ThinkingMan can certainly love chocolate too. Besides, why am I thinking of the poker chatter from last night when I'm with this guy right now?

"In fact," he continues, "my business partner and I are going to make some flamingo-shaped chocolate."

"You're in the chocolate business?"

"Lulu's Chocolates. I handle all the business deals. Which is kind of an odd twist of fate, because back in college I was so sure I was going to be an essayist."

I laugh. "Is that even a profession anymore? Wasn't that a job back in the day when there were Federalist Papers and Alexander Hamilton and all that?"

He gives me the side-eye. "Moment of truth. Are you saying that because you know Hamilton from history or from the musical?"

I shoot him a look like I'm offended. "Hey, I know Hamilton just as well as the next person." I smirk. "Obviously, from the musical. That's pretty much how we all know him these days."

"And we all know him so well. I've seen it three times."

I furrow my brow. "Here in Miami?"

He waves in the general direction of north. "Oh no, back in New York. I try to go to Broadway shows as much as I can."

"So you're in New York a lot?" I ask, wondering if his job takes him there.

He smiles. "I am. And wouldn't it be a great place to be an essayist?"

"So why did you want to be an essayist?"

"I was a philosophy major in college, so naturally I thought I would become the next great thinker."

I nod. It's all coming together finally. "That makes sense now. Hence the ThinkingMan name."

"What?"

"ThinkingMan," I repeat, because . . . hello, isn't it obvious?

"Sure. I'd consider myself a thinking man." His answer is hesitant.

"Well, I hope so."

"Well, I am."

My mind snags on details. Philosophy. Didn't Cameron say he liked philosophy? And chocolate? While it's not unusual to like chocolate, it's certainly more unique to dig philosophy.

Disconnecting now. Definitely disconnecting.

"So that's how you picked the name Thinking-Man," I add, trying desperately to connect again.

He clears his throat. "Actually, this is probably a good time to let you know my name isn't Mac, like you said earlier."

"It's not? Why did you tell me it was?" The hair on my neck stands up. What if Grams was right? He could be an ax murderer. A serial killer.

Total disconnect.

Mayday.

Abort.

I gulp. I've been catfished. Catfished by a total creepozoid criminal, and I'm about to be kidnapped. I glance right, look left. A family of four strolls ahead of us. I'll run to them. Wait, no. I'll be putting their little toddler in danger. I'll dart the other way, shouting *fire!* "I forgot I have some-place to be."

I turn, ready to jet.

"Wait. No. Sorry to throw you off. I'm Cameron. Cameron Townsend. I know you know that, but you called me Mac earlier. Just wanted to make sure you remembered from our chat."

I stop.

Blink.

I'm in an alternate universe.

The parallel worlds fold into each other.

I try to breathe evenly. "You're LuckySuit?"

His lips curve into a grin. "Yeah. Who did you think I was?"

Someone else entirely.

12

Cameron

I hold my arms out wide in a question. "Who the heck is ThinkingMan?"

Her eyes are etched with confusion. Just like I'm sure mine are. She points, practically stabbing me with her finger. "You. You're ThinkingMan."

"I just told you my name. Like I told you my name last night."

"But, but, but," she sputters. "I thought ThinkingMan was your handle. I'm Telescoper. I said it when we met, and you acted like you knew it. I'm Telescoper and you're ThinkingMan. We've chatted the last few nights." Her voice intensifies, as if she's trying to make a last-ditch point in a flagging debate.

I correct her. "We chatted *last* night. When you destroyed me in poker," I say, trying to jog her memory. How does she not recall this? "Remember? You were all sassy and said you were taking me down, and then you did, winning hand after hand."

She squeezes her eyes shut, as if she's trying the good old there's-no-place-like-home technique to wish herself out of this situation. When she opens them, she says, "But we talked about Orion Nebula and wordplay. You said *points for wordplay*."

Ah, her wordplay comment makes a bit more sense now. But little else does. "Orion Nebula is a beauty, and I'd love to check it out sometime, but we never discussed that. We talked about your multiplication marathon and your Roller Derby skills as Calcu Lass. Great name still, by the way."

She sighs heavily. "Yes, I remember discussing all that with LuckySuit. But I don't understand how you're you too. How you're the other guy as well."

I laugh, confused as a tangled mess of wires. "Me neither. Well, correction. I do understand how I'm me. But I don't understand who you've been talking to."

Her face is a portrait of frustration. "It's you on the dating site. I've been talking to you."

I shake my head, slow and easy. "I'm not on any online dating sites."

She blinks, whispering in a hush, "You're not?"

"I thought about trying it out. I got online the other night. I came *this* close to setting up a profile. But I didn't pull the trigger. I was even telling my business partner, Lulu, the other day that I'd been considering it."

"You really didn't go through with it?"

I shake my head. "No. I poked around, but in the end, I didn't do it. She even offered to set up my profile. But it never felt right."

Kristen drags a hand through her hair. "You knew about the stargazing and astronomy and asking questions though."

"Well, yeah." I'm about to add that Jeanne told me all those details, when Kristen cuts in.

"But it was *your* picture. You look just like your picture."

"My picture?" A laugh bursts from my throat. A strange *what the hell* laugh. "Someone is pretending to be me? This I need to see." I wiggle my fingers, the sign to show me the goods.

She grabs her phone, clicks on a few screens, then shoves it at me.

And there I am indeed.

Looking good.

Looking like I did on Sunday morning.

At the car auction.

The weirdness is unweirded. The confusion is de-confused. I take a deep breath. "I believe we've been catfished."

"Ya think?"

I can barely rein in a smile. "We've been pranked, Kristen." A laugh rumbles deep in my belly, moves up my chest, and spills out. I laugh harder than I've laughed in a long time. I can barely speak, and I grab her arm as if I'll topple over.

She chuckles lightly too, as if she can't quite fight it off. "Are you okay . . . whoever you are?"

I straighten, wipe the remnants of laughter away, and look her in the eye. "I'm Cameron, like I said. And it seems Jeanne was playing me, since she's the real Camera-er."

She stares at me with those wide green eyes, waiting for all the puzzle pieces to slide together. "What do you mean?"

"That picture of me on ThinkingMan's profile? Jeanne took it on Sunday. At the car auction."

Her expression transforms from perplexed, to shocked, to a new sort of awe. "Are you kidding me?"

I grab her phone, make the photo bigger, and show her where Jeanne was standing on Sunday. "There. She was right next to me. And she snapped a sneaky selfie like this." I wrap my arm around Kristen's shoulders, like Jeanne had hers around me, and mime snapping a shot.

Then I snap the photo for real. "There."

I linger for a second. Because she smells delicious. Like mangoes and pineapples. Like a tropical treat at a popsicle stand, and I would like to take a little lick of her neck. Add in a nibble on her earlobe. A kiss of her jawline.

Then, I'd kiss her lips, soft at first, then hard and properly. The kind of kiss that makes a woman swoon. That makes her melt. That's the only way a woman should ever be kissed.

But we're trying to sort out a catfishing case, so I drop my arm.

She lets out a gust of breath that tells me maybe she liked my arm around her too.

Then she laughs, full throttle, in a way that shakes her whole body to the bones. And it's incredibly sexy to watch a woman laugh so unabashedly. So shamelessly.

When she stops, she's smiling, and it's somehow brighter, richer, fuller than before.

And I still like her.

Even though I'm not sure how many conversations she's had with me, or someone else.

I show her the picture. "See? She just snipped herself out."

Kristen shakes her head in appreciation. "She is such a sneaky bird."

I smile. "And I thought I was clever with doctored birth certificates."

"A few days ago, I made her think I was going to send a formal breakup letter to the last guy she set me up with. I had her going on Saturday night, believing me."

I lift a brow. "Maybe she was trying to pull a fast one on you in retaliation?"

"Oh, she definitely wins the prank wars on this one. She's been pretending to be you and chatting with me." She shakes a fist. "I'm going to wring that dirty bird's neck when I see her again."

A knot of disappointment tightens inside me. I was hoping Kristen would be on the same page. That she was enjoying our date as much as I was. But it seems she's not sure who she's enjoyed spending time with.

"Well, maybe don't be too rough with her," I tease.

She arches a brow. "I'm going to kick her butt. And I don't mean at poker."

"You're really mad?"

She takes a deep sigh, heads to a bench at the end of the street, and plops down. I join her. "Think about it," she says. "My grandma was ThinkingMan, the guy I was chatting with. What does that make me? Some weird, strange freak who liked flirting with her . . ."

I reach for her hand, clasp it. "No, it doesn't make you anything bad at all. I suppose it simply makes her . . . clever."

She glances down at our hands. I'm holding her palm. Our fingers aren't threaded together. But still . . . she doesn't let go. She squeezes back lightly. "She really sounded like . . ."

"What did she sound like?" I try to mask my disappointment. I was honestly hoping she'd liked talking to me, not that other dude.

"She sounded like a guy who liked the same things as me. Who said all these things about opposites not attracting."

A lightbulb goes off. "Whoa. Wait a second. What did you just say?"

She drops my hand, grabs her phone, and clicks over to the conversation. "This is insanely embarrassing, but whatever. She had this whole thing about opposites not attracting."

Kristen shows me the start of the chat.

Dear Telescoper,

As you may have surmised, I'm not a big believer in the "opposites attract" theory. But I do love theories, and from your profile, I can see you do too. While I won't pretend to be someone I'm not, and I can't claim to be conversant in all things mathematical, I do love theories, debating them, dissecting them, and deconstructing them.

Also, stargazing rules. Did you know that the Andromeda Galaxy is going to crash into the Milky Way in 4.5 billion years? Of course you do. But what do you think that collision will look like?

Best,

ThinkingMan

"Damn, she's good," I say in appreciation.

"I know."

I tap the screen. "You do realize what she did

here? She used my voice. She made it sound just like me."

She tilts her head, studying me. "What do you mean?"

"At the auction, she was telling me you were single and had started online dating. I was telling her I'm not a fan of online dating because it removed chemistry and connection. And then I said I don't believe opposites attract, that I love debating all kinds of interesting topics, and that I love theories and philosophies and talking about meaningful issues. In this note, she basically parroted all the things I said."

Her jaw falls open. "Do you know what she did, then?"

"She mimicked me?"

"And she also created a perfect online persona of what I want and what I'm looking for."

And is it crazy that I want that online persona to be mine? That I want Jeanne to have stolen my traits to romance Kristen, Cyrano de Bergerac—style? "Is that so?"

She adjusts her glasses. "I don't believe opposites attract. I think they repel."

I tap my chest. "Choir. Preach it to me."

She laughs again, and if this were a real date, I'd chalk up another point. But I'm not sure what *this* is at all now. She brushes her hand lightly against my chest. "And she had you talking about all the things I like to talk about."

"Then she asked you to play her in poker against me. And when she realized we were getting along well, she set us up," I say, continuing to slide the pieces together.

Kristen scoots closer, drops her voice like we're detectives passing out clues. "That's why I don't think it was a prank, Cameron. I mean, it was. But I think she was playing matchmaker all along. She knew I only wanted to meet guys online, so she put the guy she wanted me to date online."

"And she knew I wasn't into online dating. But she wanted me to meet you. So she engineered a way for us to meet, each thinking it was exactly what we wanted—real life for me, and online for you."

Kristen scratches her head. "But she had to know we'd find out."

"Maybe she thought we wouldn't care."

"Because she figured we'd like each other and it wouldn't matter."

And I do like her. But it seems it does matter how we met. And how we didn't meet. "That must have been her grand plan."

Kristen scoffs. "That's crazy."

"Is it?"

She stares at me through her glasses. "You're fun and great and smart, and I don't know which side is up."

"I hear ya." I swallow roughly. I was hoping she'd be into me for me. And yeah, I shouldn't be bummed. I hardly know her. This is only one date.

One fun, amusing, bizarre date. One highly

entertaining online chat. One moment bursting with possibilities and potential.

And that moment seems to be fizzling.

"She really hates the idea of me online dating," Kristen adds.

"And see, I'm the opposite. I don't care for online dating. Well, not until I talked to you."

She pulls away slightly to stare at me. "But was that online?"

"I think it definitely was. We were on our phones."

"Yeah," she says, the hint of a smile tugging at her lips. But the smile fades. "It's crazy though. You live in New York. I didn't even really know who I was talking to. And it's all just a setup. It never would have worked."

"No. Never at all," I agree. She's right. But I wish she was wrong.

I sigh and figure it's best to end the date sooner rather than later.

But Kristen arches a brow, looks at me with a glint in her eyes, and I swear I see computer algorithms whirring inside her brain.

"It wouldn't. But I have a crazy idea."

13

Kristen

The first order of business is to send a note to Grams.

Me: Cameron is awesome! You were right. We're getting along so well. I can't wait to tell you everything.

Then we're off and running. We slide into his rental car, his bag with him, and drive to Miami International Airport. Once inside, we take a photo, waving with the airport sign behind us. We head all the way to security, snapping selfies as we go.

A little later, we grab our seats. More photos taken. Champagne poured. Glasses raised. "What should we toast to?" I say, a smile tipping the corners of my mouth. I'm having too much fun.

Not that there is such a thing.

Cameron stares off into the distance, as if he's thinking. For a second, it hits me—he really is ThinkingMan. He fits the bill. He talks like the man online. He seems like the man online.

How could my grandmother conjure him up so perfectly?

I blink away the thought since I don't quite know what to make of it or what to do with the wild caper we've embarked on tonight.

He meets my gaze, and those blue eyes hold mine. They shine with desire and with possibility. That look—I haven't seen it in a long time, and I like it. I like it because *I* feel it too.

He inches closer. My breath hitches from him being so near.

This is *connecting*.

"Let's toast to what comes next," he says, and the words are drenched with possibility. So much unexpected possibility that *whoosh* goes the rest of the world.

My heart flutters, and my skin sizzles as I imagine what "next" could be. Touches, kisses, sighs, moans. Butterflies, and their naughty cousins in lingerie, inhabit my chest as I clink my glass to his. "To what comes next, whatever it might be."

With my free hand, I hold up my phone and snap a photo as we move in close, cheek to cheek. I catch a faint scent of his aftershave, or maybe it's his soap. It's clean and fresh and decidedly masculine, all at once. The scent makes my stomach flip, sending a shimmy down my body on a fast track to right where I need him.

For a moment, I stop and assess the situation. That's what I do best. I apply numbers and reason. Numbers don't lie. I've felt quantifiably *more* first-date tingles with Cameron, and more intense ones too, than I have on other dates. Certainly far more than I've had on any cheese-making or carrot-pickling outings.

Obviously.

I set down my glass. He does the same.

Numbers wash away, and I let chemistry take over as I press a quick kiss to the sandpaper five-o'clock shadow stubble on his cheek. When I dust my lips to his face, I close my eyes, and a whole new zip of pleasure races across my skin, leaving a trail of sparks in its wake.

I love the scratch of his cheek.

I love the feel of his skin.

I love what it does to me.

He moves ever so slightly, and then we're looking at each other, not like two people playing a game. Not like a man and woman orchestrating a crazy idea.

We're lingering like two people who want something else.

Something we both crave. The reason we date. The reason we sift through online profiles, the reason we let our friends and family set us up, the reason we seek out another person.

For connection.

For chemistry.

And the cherry on top . . .

The prospect of a kiss.

"Kiss for the camera?" I ask. It comes out breathy, betraying all my inner longing.

I don't care.

"A kiss for the camera is necessary to pull off this caper." He makes the first move, inching closer to me. I watch him until I can't watch him anymore, until my eyes cross, and then I shut them and feel the soft whisper of his lips across mine. I gasp quietly, savoring the first touch from this man who's maybe two men, or maybe he's half of both men I liked. But even though the seesaw of Lucky-Suit and ThinkingMan threw me off, there's nothing confusing about the way his lips feel against mine.

Even though it's a staged kiss, it feels wholly real, especially as he lingers and I taste him on my lips.

He tastes like the one man I want now. The man I want a second date with. A second date we won't be having.

But oh, how I wish we could.

It's a good thing I'm sitting, because I'm melting from his lips brushing mine, from his scent flooding my nostrils, and from his hand cupping my cheek.

By all accounts, it's a modest kiss.

But tell that to my body.

To my body, his kiss feels dirty and delicious all over, like it could lead to hotel rooms after dark, to wrists pinned, to up-against-the-wall escapades.

To *all night long*.

We break apart.

He whispers, "Wow." All of those sparks turn into a fireworks show in my chest. Exploding, bursting. A *wow* from the barest kiss.

That may be the most unexpected part of today.

Because it's a wow for me too.

* * *

When we arrive at our destination, we scurry to a nearby palm tree, and we point upward. I know the *Welcome to Vegas* sign will be lit up and neon in our shot.

We high-five.

"We're pulling this off."

"We are seriously kind of amazing," I say.

He shoots me a look. "Kind of? We're just plain and simple amazing."

"Fine, fine. Have it your way. We're absolutely amazing."

"Are you ready for what comes next?"

I nod. "I'm absolutely ready."

"Positive? You don't want to go roller skate or lie on a blanket under the stars instead?"

I narrow my eyes. "I want to do both. Right now. All the time. But I want to do *this* too. Do you?"

"Just making sure," he says with a smile.

"Are you sure?"

Cameron laughs, and the sound makes my heart vault. Why do I like the sound of his laughter so much? I wish I knew. But I really, really like it.

"I'm very sure," he says with a smile, then loops his arm around my waist and yanks me close. "By the way, have I told you you're a whole lot of fun? Like, more fun than monkeys in a barrel?"

"But how does anyone know how much fun monkeys in a barrel really are?"

"I don't know. Has anyone ever put monkeys in a barrel and tried to have fun with them?"

"I hope not. That doesn't seem like it would be fun for the monkeys."

"And we really should be nice to monkeys," he says, then presses a kiss to my nose.

I sigh into the kiss and whisper, "I'm having fun too. More fun than if I was watching *Cupid* stream online."

He arches a brow in a question.

I wave a hand. "It's this old TV show. I keep hoping someday it'll stream online. Let's skedaddle, and we can discuss Camus, you philosophy major, you."

His eyes twinkle. "Don't get me excited, Kristen."

"Camus gets you excited?"

"Almost as much as Descartes."

As we hop in the car, racing to our next destination, I flash back over the night. Over the kiss and the champagne, the fun and the conversations. The way we get along so weirdly well, the way we both jumped on this crazy idea.

And it wasn't an algorithm that brought us together.

It was a person.

Or maybe it was us.

* * *

At the chapel, we say hello to an Elvis impersonator and we snag a photo with him. Then he does the deed.

"I now pronounce you man and wife."

With those words, all I can think is we are getting so even they're going to need a new word for "even."

"You may kiss the bride."

"Take our picture, please, would you, Elvis?"

Elvis nods as Cameron hands him his camera.

Cameron cups my cheeks, brings my face to his, and plants the most delicious kiss on my lips.

He's gentle at first. A tender sweep of his lips.

A brush against mine. Just enough for tingles to spread down my arms, leaving a trail of goose-bumps in their wake.

I feel a little swoony, a little shimmery, as flutters race across my body.

Then, he kicks it up a notch. He's more insistent, a touch greedy.

And holy hell, I like greedy from him. I like it a lot. His kiss becomes demanding as his hands clasp my face, and his mouth explores mine. Tongues, lips, teeth. He kisses with an ownership, like he wants me more than he ever expected.

It's the same for me, I want to say. It's absolutely the same for me.

And I don't need to speak those words, because our bodies are talking. He tugs me closer, deepening the kiss.

The game is all the way on, and his lips devastate mine as he kisses me with a delicious intensity.

I rise on tiptoe, thread my hands around his neck, and kiss him hard. Like he's mine. Like he belongs to me tonight. And that's how this feels. Like I get to have him in this moment.

A fevered, frenzied moment punctuated by moans, and groans, and needy sighs. By kisses that can't possibly end. By a connection neither one of us wants to break because it feels so damn good.

Everywhere.

He doesn't just kiss my lips. His mouth travels along my neck, visiting the hollow of my throat. Dear god, that's spectacular. His lips on my throat send an electric charge straight through me, and I'm operating at a high voltage. He senses my reaction. I can feel his naughty smile against my skin as he kisses his way up my neck now, on a path for my ear where he nibbles on my earlobe.

And I squirm.

The good kind of squirm.

The kind where my knees are jelly from the nip of his teeth right there.

This kiss hits me all over—toes, knees, belly.

It sizzles through me, frying my brain and filling it with thoughts of where it could lead to.

Kiss me everywhere. Kiss me all over. Kiss every inch of my skin.

These thoughts run rampant in my brain, surprising me.

Stunning me with the depth of my response to him.

We hit it off instantly online, and in spite of all the mix-ups and all the puzzle pieces that didn't quite fit earlier, I feel far more connected to him in person than logic dictates I should.

Than the strange circumstances of this most bizarre date say I should.

I feel connected to him. I like him. And I don't want this to end.

But we have to disconnect.

I break the kiss, pressing a palm to his chest. "We should stop before . . ."

"Before it goes too far?" he asks.

"Yes. Exactly."

"We better. Because *far* would feel far too good."

"It would feel amazing."

* * *

Later, much later, it rains.

It seems fitting, especially since it's time to say good night. There's an empty ache in my chest.

I didn't expect to feel a hollow spot as I said goodbye to Cameron.

But the ache is real, and it hurts as I stand curbside. The rain falls, so I grab my red umbrella from my purse and open it, holding it above us.

"One more picture. Just for me," he says.

I smile faintly, and he tugs me closer and snaps a close-up. He tucks his phone away and hands me a rose.

"Where you'd find a rose?"

He wiggles an eyebrow. "I have my ways."

"No, seriously. Where did you find a rose?"

Laughing, he tells me, "Elvis gave me one to give to you."

"Well, thank you to Elvis."

Cameron runs a thumb across my jawline. "One more kiss? Just for me. No cameras."

I smile, and it seems to reach to my toes, the ends of my hair, my fingertips. "No cameras. Just us."

"Just us," he echoes as he slides a hand into my

hair, brings me close, and whispers, "I'm so glad she tricked us."

"Me too."

As I hold the rose, he kisses me goodbye, and this one is bittersweet.

It's full of promise. It speaks of where those kisses could have led. To how *far* they would have gone. To the kind of nights that might have unfurled between us.

But it also tells stories that must end, since the story of our one and only date is marching toward its inevitable final line.

His lips linger on mine, the barest of touches, like he can't bear for this to end.

Same for me.

"One more," I whisper, and I'm the greedy one.

But he obliges, banding an arm around my waist, hauling me close, and planting one helluva goodbye on my lips, like the kind a sailor gives his woman when he leaves.

Then he does just that.

He leaves.

He takes off on a plane to Vegas for real this time, and I run my finger over my lips, remembering.

I go home, set the rose in a vase, and crash. I'm glad too that Grams tricked us, but I'm also not, because I wanted to believe this was something real.

14

Jeanne
  Earlier that day

As she finished up the Camaro, her phone dinged.

Wiping her hands on a red bandana, she took the device from her back pocket, clicked opened the text, and nearly squealed when she saw that Kristen and Cameron were having such a good time.

Kristen: We had a blast! We're going to spend the whole evening together since we're taking a little trip.

Jeanne had never been so pleased.

Grandmas always knew best. With seventy-five years on this earth, she was simply right.

They were so dang perfect for each other. All they needed was somebody to bring them together, even if it took a little subterfuge. No harm, no foul. Besides, they were both so stubborn in their own ways. That was why they'd needed her—to smush them together as only she could. So what if she'd had to pretend to be Cameron for a few nights? All for a good cause, and clearly she'd made the right call.

Jeanne: I knew you'd hit it off! So thrilled. I won't say I told you so.

Kristen: You did tell me so. I have to turn my phone off now, but we'll be there in five hours and I promise to send you a barrage of photos!

Jeanne: Wait! Five hours for what—

A new message landed, and she clicked on it, opening a photo. Her eyebrows lifted. They were toasting each other on a plane? In first-class seats? What was that all about? And where were they going that took five hours to get there?

Yet they were having fun and already flying together.

Perhaps she was a better matchmaker than she'd thought.

With a satisfied grin, she went inside and prepped for her own date, grateful that Joe had had the gumption to call her up after the auction. They'd already gone to a classic car show the other afternoon in South Beach, and they'd had such a fantastic time that he'd asked her to go to the racetrack tonight. That man was a handsome devil, and she was delighted that he didn't seem to care that she was fifteen years older. Did that make her a cougar?

She roared at herself in the mirror and brandished her cougar claws.

"So be it."

She swiped on mascara, some lipstick, and headed to the racetrack.

* * *

Her phone dinged once more as a hot green sports car cheetahed its way around the track.

"You waiting for a girlfriend to give you an out?" Joe teased.

She patted his leg. "Puh-leaze. If I didn't like you, I'd tell you to your face."

He flashed an *I'm waiting* smile. "Well?"

"You know I like you. The question is, how much do I like you?" She smiled.

"I'd like to know how much."

"So would I," she said flirtily then grabbed her phone. "Let me see if it's Kristen."

She flinched when the photo loaded. What were they doing *there*? Were they truly in Sin City?

"Look," she whispered, showing him the picture of Kristen and Cameron beneath the Vegas sign.

"Seems they like each other. Just wanted to get away for a night in Vegas."

She knew Cameron had been heading to Vegas for work, but had Kristen gone along with him? Didn't she have to work the next day? Vegas was . . . well, a five-hour flight.

Her phone buzzed once more.

She startled.

And what was this? Elvis? And a chapel?

She froze. Kristen, her sweet, darling, clever Kristen, had fallen so quickly she'd eloped in Las Vegas?

She shook her head, like there was water in her ears. "She was supposed to look at urban art, get a cup of coffee, and maybe have a kiss," she blurted out.

Joe cocked his head, stared at her quizzically. "Come again?"

She shoved the screen at him, showing him the string of texts. "They eloped! They ran off to Vegas and got married."

Joe nearly spat out his drink as he gawked at the photos. "What is up with kids today?"

"I knew they'd like each other, but this seems a touch extreme."

"Just a little."

But at the same time, she couldn't help but pat herself on the back. It was extreme, but sometimes you just knew.

15

Cameron

As the hotel executive shares his ideas for where he wants to introduce a Lulu's Chocolates cart in the lobby of The Luxe, a newer Vegas resort, I listen furiously, giving him my undivided attention as best I can.

Because my attention these last twenty-four hours has definitely been divided.

I'm here, chatting in the lobby of this hotel.

But my mind is back in Miami, running around the city as we pranked Kristen's grandma, making her think we loved our setup so much we'd run off to Vegas to tie the knot.

Photoshop for the win.

Right now, I'm hardly thinking of photo-doctoring software that made us look like we were in a first-class cabin or under the famous Vegas sign. Nor am I thinking of poker chip–themed chocolate, though I know I should be.

I'm remembering that last kiss.

An airport kiss.

The kind that makes you want more. That makes you wish one person wasn't going one way and the other person going another.

Heck, I'd love to be hopping on a plane to Miami again tonight, rather than returning to New York.

When the meeting ends and the exec tells me the deal looks good, I ought to be happy.

Too bad when I hop on a plane that evening, I'm not exactly jumping for joy.

As I fly over the country, I tell myself it was only one date. "Get over it, man."

16

Kristen

The next morning, I hit the roller rink at the crack of dawn, working out on my skates. I have an hour before I need to be at work, so I skate then return home, ready to shower.

Grams pounces on me the second I walk through the doorway.

She grabs my wrist. "Tell me everything."

I clasp my hand to my chest, flutter my eyelids, and do my best starry-eyed impression. "Oh, it was magical, and I'm in love."

Her eyes twinkle. "You are?"

The funny thing is . . . it doesn't feel far from possible. Not today, but down the road. Maybe in a few months, I could honestly see myself falling for Cameron.

That's what doesn't add up.

It's illogical. It's irrational. It's ridiculous.

But it's also why my heart weighs heavy.

Grams stares at me, studying my hands. "Where's your ring?"

I walk inside, drop my bag on the couch, set my phone on the table, and turn around. I don't have the energy to keep up the prank anymore. I've pulled her leg and gotten her goat. It was a blast, and yet, I'm sadder than I want to be.

I shrug. "It was a joke. We didn't go to Vegas to get married. We spent the evening running around Miami, taking pictures under palm trees and then photoshopping them to look like the Vegas sign, an airplane, and so on."

Her eyes bulge. "What? How?"

"We bought champagne and glasses, went to the monorail, parked ourselves in the seats, and toasted on it." I don't add that we kissed on the monorail and that it was some kind of magic that didn't need an ounce of retouching in a photo. "Then Cameron photoshopped it to look like we were on an airplane."

Her jaw clangs to the floor, cash register–style. "You didn't." Her tone says she can't believe she's been had, yet she's also wildly impressed.

"We did. Then we snagged the Elvis impersonator on the beach and went to a chapel here on South Beach, and we pretended to get married."

"Why did you do all that?"

I park my hands on my hips. "Why did you catfish me?"

She tuts. "I would hardly call it catfishing."

"I would precisely call it catfishing."

She squares her shoulders. "I knew he was right for you."

"He's great," I say, unable to mask the affection I feel for him. "But I want to make my own choices. You had me going. You made me feel . . . a little foolish."

Her expression falters, and she frowns. "But you liked him."

"Yeah, I did. And I do. But I also felt kind of stupid when I learned it had all been a ruse."

"It wasn't all a ruse. You loved chatting with him during poker, didn't you?"

I squeeze her arm. "I did, but don't you see? I want to make my own choices, and I want you to respect them."

She exhales, nods, and licks her lips. "I'm sorry if I overstepped. I just thought he was a good man for you, and it was the only way I could get you to meet him. Plus, I didn't make anything up—everything I told you was from conversations I'd had with the real Cameron over poker. So technically, you were talking to him—just through me."

"Like you're a medium now?"

She snaps her fingers and grins. "Exactly. I was channeling him."

"You made it sound so real," I say, a little sad. "I wished it'd been him. And I wish you'd just asked me to go on a blind date."

"After the pickle embalmer and the cheesy cheesemaker, you'd have said no."

"True," I admit.

"Aren't you glad you said yes?"

I scoff. "I didn't say yes!"

"You can't think of ThinkingMan as me. He was Cameron. It was all him."

I shoot her a skeptical look. "It was actually all you."

"Technically, but the profile was based on him, and when I knew the two of you actually liked each other after your poker chat, I figured it was fine to set you up on a date."

"What if I hadn't liked him playing poker?"

"But I knew you would."

"What if I hadn't?" I press.

"Well . . . I don't know," she admits. Then she reaches out, wraps her arms around me. "I'm sorry if I was out of line. I want you to be happy and to find the right person. I thought you'd like him."

I rest my cheek against her shoulder, catching a glimpse of the rose in the vase, fading after only one night, as roses do. "I did like him, and you were right. But here's the trouble." I separate and meet her eyes. "He's gone. He doesn't live here."

She waves a hand dismissively. "What's distance when love's involved?"

"One, we're not involved. Two, it's a big thing. Three—"

"Just get on a plane and see him."

I raise a finger. "Do not secretly book me on a flight. Or him. Do you understand?"

She laughs and raises her right hand. "I promise."

Then she mutters, "For now."

* * *

Later that night, I open my tablet, and I'm tempted to check out the online dating site. But the guy I want to talk to isn't there.

The next morning I find a text on my phone.

It's not from ThinkingMan.

It's not from LuckySuit.

It's from Cameron.

17

Cameron

I'm not over it.

Not over her.

Not interested in getting over the best date of my life.

I have no agenda, no notion of what's next. But as I walk down Sixth Avenue, the warm summer breeze wrapping around me, I picture the montage of moments I want right now.

And all the shots are of Kristen.

I decide to stop thinking about texting her . . . and text her.

Cameron: Question. When you skated, were you as feared on the rink as you were at the blackboard?

Kristen: But of course. I made opponents cower.

Cameron: I'm not in the least bit surprised. Do you still skate, and when you do, do you wear those socks that go to your knees?

Kristen: You mean . . . wait for it . . . knee-high socks?

Cameron: Yes, those.

Kristen: I do. Got a thing for knee-high socks?

Cameron: Interesting question. I'd love to find out. It would be helpful if you could send me a photo of you in full skater regalia, knee-high socks and all, and then I could answer you honestly.

Kristen: All in the name of research and learning, of course?

Cameron: Of course.

I wait patiently, threading through the morning crowds as I head to meet Lulu. Two blocks later, my phone buzzes and I'm rewarded with a photo.

There. Is. A. God.

It's a picture of Kristen—legs only. She's wearing white knee-high socks with purple stripes.

Those legs in those socks. Kill me now.

Cameron: Do you realize you make socks sexy?

Kristen: Why, thank you. You make . . . polo shirts sexy?

Cameron: You remembered what I wore. :)

Kristen: Or maybe I'm looking at some of the photos we took . . .

Okay, now I have a city-wide grin stealing the real estate on my face.

Cameron: Maybe I've been doing that too. Good thing we took so many pictures.

Kristen: Do you have a favorite?

I stop at the crosswalk, click over to my photo folder, and find the last shot. The one I snapped at the airport. I didn't photoshop this picture. It's just us, before the night ended. I send it to her.

Kristen: Ah, I like that one too. And now I have one more to look at.

Cameron: I might have looked at it a few times already.

Kristen: I'm catching up to you right now on that tally. By the way, what are you doing today?

Cameron: Contemplating chocolate, business deals, and how to grow wings and/or learn to Apparate.

Kristen: And what exactly would you do if you could Apparate? Inquiring minds want to know.

Cameron: Take you out, pretend we were at the Taj Mahal, maybe add Mt. Everest or a Buddhist temple behind us, possibly even the Leaning Tower of Pisa. Or we could visit Monkey Jungle and mock up a picture of us in a barrel testing the baseline of fun. Other options—take you to a bookstore and get lost in books on philosophy. Go to a concert and decide whether indie is better than pop, or just debate it all night long. Take you to a roller rink and watch you skate in those knee socks, then take them off . . .

Kristen: Where do I sign up?

Cameron: You good with all that?

Kristen: With every single thing. But you know what I like most?

Cameron: Do tell.

Kristen: Talking to you as you.

Cameron: I like that too. More than I want to.

But now I have to end the conversation. I say goodbye and head into the shop, feeling both better and worse.

18

Kristen

I text him the next afternoon.

Kristen: Today my hair is purple. I ate eggplant for lunch.

Cameron: I've got an eggplant right here for you.

Kristen: *facepalm*

Cameron: You did walk right into that.

Kristen: I did. I totally did.

* * *

That night he texts me.

Cameron: By the way, I've been meaning to ask about the Orion Nebula.

Kristen: IS THIS YOU?

Cameron: YES. WHY?

Kristen: You know this is how I was catfished! The Orion Nebula was the bait.

Cameron: I'll prove it's me.

I wait, and his picture appears on my phone. His face. Then his . . . feet? Is he actually wearing . . .?

Kristen: Are you wearing Crocs?

Cameron: Yes.

Kristen: Why would you show me Crocs and, more importantly, why would you wear them?

Cameron: To answer the latter, they're comfortable. To answer the former, to prove it's me.

Kristen: That proves this is you?

Cameron: It proves I'm me because if I were someone else impersonating me, he'd never humble himself by showing Crocs. I'm showing you who I really am.

Kristen: A Croc wearer?

Cameron: Yes, do you still like me?

My smile is contagious. They're grinning in the next county, and they caught it from me.

Kristen: Yes. But for the love of pi and the golden ratio, please never show them to me in person so I don't have to bleach my eyeballs. Deal?

Cameron: Deal. Especially the in-person part.

Kristen: Also, is it so obvious l like you that you knew even Crocs wouldn't ruin it?

Cameron: Call me crazy, but I like obvious on this count. In fact, I like it a lot. And I like you—a whole helluva lot.

Kristen: Same . . . it's totally the same. Even in Crocs.

Cameron: Now, back to the Orion Nebula. Evidently, the first me, who wasn't me but rather based on me, talked to you about it. But I wanted to look at it tonight, and since you're a stargazer, I was hoping you could give me some guidance.

And my heart goes thud. It falls to the floor, beating for him, like a silly, lust-struck fool.

Kristen: I'd love to. But it's easier to talk it through on the phone.

Three seconds later, my phone rings.

"What a cheap excuse to get me to call," he teases.

"But it worked."

"I'm easy like that."

I go to the deck, stare at the night sky, and tell him how to find the constellation. When we're done searching millions of miles away, we talk about music and our friends. I learn about Lulu, and I tell him about Piper, and the ache in my chest grows.

But so do the feelings.

They balloon.

"What are we doing?" I ask.

He sighs, a little sadly. "I don't know. I shouldn't be calling you like this. It makes everything harder."

"I know. Talking to you till all hours makes it harder."

"It makes me wish I were there."

I lean back in the chair, closing my eyes. "What would you do if you were?"

"Kiss you." His voice is a sexy rumble.

I hum. "Where?"

"Your lips, the hollow of your throat, your earlobe, where you like to be nipped."

I shiver. "Do I like to have my earlobe nibbled on?"

"Oh, you absolutely do. And I'd kiss you for hours."

"I'd squirm for hours," I whisper.

"I like all the sounds you make when I kiss you. I'd like to know what other sounds you make."

Flames. I go up in flames. "I suspect you'd be cataloguing a whole lot of noises."

A soft chuckle comes from his end of the line, followed by a sexy sigh. "I'd like to kiss you everywhere, Kristen."

And I die. From the visual my brain helpfully assembled. From the shiver that rushed down my belly thanks to that image. And from the possibility of his mouth exploring me everywhere.

When we hang up, I'm lonelier than when we started.

* * *

It would have been smarter to stop, but we don't. We keep going over the next few weeks, as I work and see my friends, as he works and travels more for business.

Every night, we talk.

Every day, we text.

Every time, the math geek in me craves a solution. We are one side of the equation, and I don't know how to solve for x with all these miles between us.

I long to know what's on the other side of the equal sign.

One day when I return home from work, I find a package waiting outside my door. Bending, I pick up the padded manila envelope. Once inside my condo, I slide open the envelope, then I shriek.

Oops.

I'd shrieked so loudly that Grams opens her door seconds later.

"Cockroach, gator, or dragonfly?"

Laughing, I shake my head, clutching the package to my chest. "Neither. It's *Cupid*. DVDs of *Cupid*."

"That Jeremy Piven show? Who sent them?"

I can't wipe the dopey grin off my face. "Cameron."

She arches a brow knowingly. "Told you so."

I pluck the card from inside, opening it. *"Where there's a will, there's a way. I tracked these down for you. I hope you enjoy every single second of them. The only thing better would be if you were wearing knee-high socks and curled up next to me on the couch."*

He's right.

That's the only thing that would make this better.

The next day I send him a gift. One that lets him know how much I like this one.

19

Cameron

"What do you think? Great name for the new line?"

I blink up at Lulu. Shoot. What did she just tell me was her idea for the new line of chocolate?

I was too busy replaying last night's conversation with Kristen, when we listed all the things we could do in either a Ferrari or a Bugatti.

News flash—driving *wasn't* that high up.

Still, Lulu deserves an answer, and since she's aces at names, I take a wild guess that she's devised a fantastic one. "Brilliant name," I say, leaning against the counter in the shop. It's quiet right now. There's a lull in the afternoon traffic.

She shoots me a thumbs-up. "Fantastic. Toe Jam Chocolate it will be."

I adopt a straight face, though I cringe inside. "Excellent."

She shakes her head. "You are so busted."

"Please, I knew you were putting me on."

She shakes her head, poking my chest. "You. Did. Not."

"Did. So."

"You lie."

I shrug. "Fine, you caught me. I was drifting into Daydream Land."

"You've been spending a lot of time in Daydream Land since your Miami trip with Kristen."

I sigh heavily. "I know, I know."

"Heck, that weekend you guys took me to the Hamptons, you were texting her the whole time," she says, reminding me of the trip a bunch of us took Lulu on when she needed to sort out the complexities of her love life. I *might* have been talking to Kristen a whole lot that weekend. And the next week. And the next one. And telling Lulu about her. "Which makes me wonder," she adds, "why are you still here?"

"Where should I be?"

Lulu stares sharply. "Not here."

I shake my head. "I'm not doing something crazy."

"Why not? That's what love is."

"This was just a date."

"It seems like it's one fantastic date that's lasted a few weeks."

I shrug in admission. She's not wrong. "Maybe it has."

"And that brings me to my big question."

I furrow my brow. "What's that?"

Before she can answer, though, the bell above the door rings and the UPS man strides in, handing her a package.

"Must be supplies," I say, offhand.

Lulu smirks as she looks at the front of the envelope. "Supplies for you, lover boy."

My interest is piqued. "And why do you say that?" I ask as the man leaves.

Lulu holds a package behind her back. "This might as well be tied with a satin bow."

"But it's not tied with a satin bow, is it?"

She waves it above her head. "It's from your mystery woman. *Kristen.*"

My heart thumps faster. I have no clue what Kristen sent me, but whatever it is, I want it. I reach for the package.

Lulu holds it behind her back.

I roll my eyes. "We are not playing these games."

"Promise me something."

"What on earth do you want me to promise you?"

She tells me what she wants me to do after I open the package. I laugh in disbelief. "That's bonkers."

She shakes her head. "That's what you told me to do when I was all up in the air over Leo."

I shoot her a quizzical look. "I don't believe *that* is exactly what I told you to do."

She waves her hand. "Just open it."

Like a college prospect waiting for a scholarship notice, I rip open the envelope. And then I grin. Then the grin grows entirely naughty when I read Kristen's note.

Lulu shakes a finger at me. "Don't break your promise."

I don't plan to. I definitely don't plan to.

* * *

Later that night, Jeanne texts me with an idea. But I've beaten her to it.

Cameron: I'm on it already.

20

Kristen

Piper taps her chin, considering the lavender dress at the bridal shop. "So much lavender. I wish the bride chose yellow. I have twenty lavender dresses."

I arch a brow. "Twenty? That seems an exaggeration."

"Come to Manhattan. Check out my closet. I solemnly swear I have twenty."

As Piper holds up the dress to her mirrored reflection, I sink onto the plush pink chair. "I'll stow away in your bag. Go back with you."

She spins around, looking at me with sharp eyes. "You could."

I scoff. "Hide out in your bag?"

"No, goofball. Come back to New York with me."

"You're right. I don't need a job. I'll leave my condo. And my family."

"For. The. Weekend."

"Then what happens after the weekend?"

She taps her chin. "Gee, I don't know. Fly up another weekend if it works out."

"Just jet back and forth from Miami to New York?"

She nods exaggeratedly. "Yeah. It's called a long-distance relationship. You do know it's been done before? You didn't invent this scenario of falling for a guy who lives a thousand miles away."

"Thanks for clarifying. I thought I had."

"It's the modern age. People meet online. They date long-distance. They make it work."

"That's a lot to make work."

"And how many evenings have you been talking or texting him on the phone all night long?"

I cast my gaze down, grumbling, "The last several."

"And I bet some of those texts weren't entirely safe for work."

"I did not sext him. I didn't send any nudes."

She arches a brow.

I huff. "I sent him a shot of my legs. But it was a tasteful shot."

"I've no doubt he wants a taste of you."

I laugh, but my stomach is swooping, because I'd like that too. "Maybe," I say noncommittally.

She laughs, sets the dress on a hook, and

strides over to me. She lifts my chin. "You could get on a plane to New York and surprise him, and I bet he'd be ecstatic."

"That seems a little presumptuous."

"Then ask him if you should . . . *presume*."

But can I ask him that? Are we at that point? I marinate on Piper's advice as I return home, then I reread the last few nights of texts.

I stare at the photo from our date.

I close my eyes and I recall how it felt.

I open my eyes and grab my phone.

Kristen: This might be crazy, but is there any chance you might want company this weekend? Or want to be my company this weekend?

He doesn't reply.

And I do my best to pretend that doesn't equal one very sad Kristen.

21

Cameron

The car rumbles through the streets, and in the back seat, I reread my most recent chat with Jeanne.

Jeanne: I'm keeping her busy till you arrive.

Cameron: You're a good woman.

Jeanne: Also, I beat you with a full house.

Cameron: It's about time.

Jeanne: Hey, be nice to the little old lady.

Cameron: As if that description fits you at all.

Ten minutes later, my Uber arrives at my destination. I thank the driver and bound up the steps, then knock on the door.

For a second, maybe more, I wonder if this is crazy. If I've gone insane, presumptuous, and all kinds of soft inside for trying to pull off this surprise.

Maybe I have.

Maybe I'm jumping off the nutty end of the diving board.

Maybe that's okay.

Hope rises in me. A big balloon of it. Nerves expand too, relentlessly.

But what's life without a big chance now and then? After all, she's worth the risk.

Kristen opens the door. Her chestnut hair is piled high in a messy bun, her glasses are sliding down her nose, and her cute pink skirt makes me think very bad things.

Her expression, though, is priceless.

It's hope meets wild hope.

It's *Is this really happening?*

It matches mine.

She parts her lips to speak, but I go first.

I smack my forehead. "My bad. You texted me and asked if I wanted company this weekend. Figured I'd tell you in person that the answer is yes."

She grabs my shirt collar and yanks me inside,

crushing my lips with hers in a hot, searing kiss. The door isn't even closed, and I don't care. She's on fire, devouring me, and I want to be burned. My head is a haze, and my body is rocketing to five-alarm levels.

Then she lets go.

"Whoa. Why'd you stop kissing me? You should do more of that. Never stop kissing me. Also, do it all night long."

She laughs and kicks the door closed. "All night long can be arranged. Also, this is perfect timing. My grams just left about ten seconds ago."

"Good. I told her to keep you occupied till I arrived."

"Wait. Did she engineer this too?"

I laugh as I slide my hands around her waist. "No, but she did tell me she thought I ought to get my butt down here. And I told her I was already on it."

She ropes her arms around my neck. "Good. Because I like your butt. Also, you had me worried."

I tug her closer. "Woman, when you send me a deck of cards with a note that says *Want to play strip poker sometime?* I am on it. I booked the next flight out of town to see you. Yes, maybe Lulu made me promise that I would get on a plane to see you, but it was all I could think about anyway."

She brushes a kiss to my lips. "Maybe let's stop talking and thinking and texting, and start doing."

That I can do.

I thread a hand in her hair and seal my mouth to hers. It's one of those slow burn kisses, the kind that takes its time, heats you up, and warms you inside and out.

But it's only slow burn for so long.

Because weeks of longing? Late-night phone calls? Flirty, dirty texts? And the kisses we shared on that first date?

The time for slow burn is over after one delicious minute of soft, gentle, open-mouthed kisses.

My circuits go haywire, and my desire rockets to sky high.

I grab her ass, lift her up, help her hook her legs around my hips, and then I carry her to the couch.

"Kiss you everywhere?" I ask, arching a brow, as I tug off my shirt. "I believe that was one of your requests?"

Her eyes blaze, and she's stripping at the speed of light too. There goes the shirt, the bra, and hallelujah. My brain is officially fried because . . . breasts.

"Yes, but right now, I kind of need something else."

"And what would that be?"

She sits up, reaches for my jeans, and makes her intentions clear. "You naked, fucking me."

What do you know? Her intentions match mine. "I aim to deliver on all your needs."

A few more seconds, and that pretty pink skirt pools on the floor, and my boxer briefs join it.

She reaches for my shoulders, bringing me close, whispering, "Hi."

"Hi," I say, as I roll on a condom.

"Also, please get inside me right now."

I laugh. "You are so damn direct and it's a hell of a turn on."

Her eyebrows wiggle as her hand darts down, clasping my erection. "I can tell. You are definitely turned on."

I groan from the red-hot pleasure, the wild thrill of her hands on me. Then, I groan from the sheer perfection of sliding inside her. This woman I adore. The woman I crave. And the woman I want badly.

She lets out the sexiest sigh in the entire galaxy as I fill her, and then she arches up into me, gripping, moving, owning her pleasure.

She's so alluring, so unabashed as she seeks the right angle, the right friction, then as she asks me to go a little faster, a little harder.

"You're going to kill me," I murmur.

"Don't die till we both come," she says, then she shudders, and lets loose a fantastic *oh god*.

My own lust shoots higher, but I stave off my finish, needing to get her there first. Needing to make sure she's all good.

And judging from her trembles and moans, from the flush in her cheeks, the part of her lips, she is way more than good.

So am I, in fact.

I'm great as her body quakes, tightening around me, then she cries out.

And that's my cue to follow her there.

We lay sated and spent, but not for long. There is kissing, and cuddling, and showering.

And then there is even more kissing.

Everywhere.

I give her what she wants, and she gives in to the sensations, wrapping her legs around me, moaning, groaning, and calling my name as I bring her there again with my mouth.

That's what we do all weekend.

And we make plans to do it again the next one.

I'm not going to let a little thing like distance stand in the way any longer. Life is complicated; love is even more so.

But there is nearly always a solution.

This is ours—we're making it work.

EPILOGUE

Cameron
A few months later

My phone flashes with a text. The words "hot tip" scream at me.

Jeanne: Word on the street is there's a seized red Ferrari coming up for auction this weekend. Maybe if you're nice to Joe, he'll hold it for you.

Cameron: Maybe if *you're* nice to Joe, he'll hold it for me.

Jeanne: I'm always good to Joe.

I roll my eyes and show the phone to Kristen, who's curled up with me on her couch on a lazy Sunday morning.

"Once a dirty bird, always a dirty bird," she says, then tugs me in for another kiss.

I'm all too happy to oblige. But there are things to discuss, so I pull back, running my finger down her nose.

"So . . . should I get the car?"

She lifts a brow. "What would you do with a car in Manhattan?"

It's an excellent question.

I tap my chin as if deep in thought. "True. When you come see me in New York, we spend most of our time in bed anyway."

She swats me. "Not true. We went to museums, and we walked across the Brooklyn Bridge, and we went to the planetarium, and we took pictures in front of Lincoln Center's fountain. But we were never in a car, Cameron."

I run my fingers through her hair. "We were never in a car in Manhattan . . ." I trail off, waiting for her to get my meaning.

"Right. And . . .?"

"But we do have to use a car . . . *here*."

She sits up straighter. "What are you saying? That you want a Ferrari to drive around in when you come visit me every other weekend?"

I shrug, grinning.

"Fine. But that seems like quite an indulgence."

I crack up. "I like indulgences. You're an indulgence." I press a kiss to her forehead then cup her cheek, meeting her gaze. "But what if it wasn't an indulgence? What if, say, I needed a car to get around town more regularly?"

Her face freezes. She goes stock-still, then she speaks in a whisper. "What are you saying?"

I can't resist toying with her logical head. "Work the problem, Kristen. What's the solution to the long-distance problem of you and me that would merit a car?"

She licks her lips. "Are you saying . . .?"

I shake my head. "I'm not saying. I'm asking. Or rather, I'd like you to ask me."

I smile, waiting.

She takes a deep breath, trembling. "Do you want to move in with me?"

"Why, I thought you'd never ask."

"But what about your job?"

"I'll run it from here. I'll make it work. I'll go back to New York from time to time. But I can't take being away from you a minute longer."

"Have I ever told you I love you more than the Milky Way?"

Her smile is wider than the galaxy.

* * *

Kristen

. . .

I'm cheering Cameron on at the auction. So is Grams. She's by Joe's side, since she's been helping him run it from time to time over the last few months.

"They're a perfect couple," I say to my mom, who wanted to come along today.

My mom hums, nodding like she has a secret up her sleeve. "They truly are. It's like they were meant to be together."

"What's that smile all about?"

She tilts her head and grins wider. "Just that I had a feeling all along about them."

"Right, that's what you said."

She clasps her hand to her chest. "Oh, allow me to clarify. It was more than a feeling."

"What are you saying?"

"I'm saying I might have a little cupid in me too." She blows on her red fingernails.

"Is that so?"

She shimmies her shoulders. "I met him at the hairdresser's and had a hunch he was right for her. So I started sending her to the auctions."

I squeeze her arm. "You little matchmaker, you."

She winks. "And you know what that means, my little genius?"

"No, what does it mean?"

"Put two and two together."

"Four?" I ask playfully.

She shakes her head. "It means I'm essentially responsible for you and Cameron getting together too. If I hadn't sent Grams here, she'd never have met him. And now look at the two of you."

I look at my guy as he bids and wins a hot red sports car. Then I turn to my mom. "I do owe you a thank-you. You knew exactly what I needed to be happy."

She shakes her head. "No, I simply hoped you'd find someone you loved. Someone you connected with. You made all that happiness happen on your own."

That afternoon, Cameron drives off the lot in his new sports car, looking all kinds of sexy behind the wheel, with me in the passenger seat.

He drapes an arm over my shoulder. "What do you say we go drive around my new city and buy towels or shaving cream or whatever it is that I'll need to live here?"

"Nothing says sexy like driving your hot new Ferrari to Bed Bath & Beyond."

We drive off into the sunset.

Two wild cards that turned into a perfect match.

If you enjoyed this novella and want to read Lulu's love story, please check out *Birthday Suit*. Piper's love story is told in *Never Have I Ever*, available now.

MOST VALUABLE PLAYBOY, a sexy multi-week USA Today Bestselling sports romance! And its companion sports romance, MOST LIKELY TO SCORE!

THE V CARD, a USA Today Bestselling sinfully sexy romantic comedy!

WANDERLUST, a USA Today Bestselling contemporary romance!

COME AS YOU ARE, a Wall Street Journal and multi-week USA Today Bestselling contemporary romance!

PART-TIME LOVER, a multi-week USA Today Bestselling contemporary romance!

UNBREAK MY HEART, an emotional second chance USA Today Bestselling contemporary romance!

BEST LAID PLANS, THE FEEL GOOD FACTOR, NOBODY DOES IT BETTER and UNZIPPED, in the Lucky in Love series of USA Today and WSJ Bestselling romances!

The Heartbreakers! The USA Today and WSJ Bestselling rock star series of standalone!

The New York Times and USA Today Bestselling Seductive Nights series including *Night After Night, After This Night,* and *One More Night*

And the two standalone

romance novels in the Joy Delivered Duet, *Nights With Him* and Forbidden Nights, both New York Times and USA Today Bestsellers!

Sweet Sinful Nights, Sinful Desire, Sinful Longing and Sinful Love, the complete New York Times Bestselling high-heat romantic suspense series that spins off from Seductive Nights!

Playing With Her Heart, a

USA Today bestseller, and a sexy Seductive Nights spin-off standalone! (Davis and Jill's romance)

21 Stolen Kisses, the USA Today Bestselling forbidden new adult romance!

Caught Up In Us, a New York Times and

USA Today Bestseller! (Kat and Bryan's romance!)

Pretending He's Mine, a Barnes & Noble and

iBooks Bestseller! (Reeve & Sutton's romance)

My USA Today bestselling

No Regrets series that includes

The Thrill of It

(Meet Harley and Trey)

and its sequel

Every Second With You

My New York Times and USA Today

Bestselling Fighting Fire series that includes

Burn For Me

(Smith and Jamie's romance!)

Melt for Him

(Megan and Becker's romance!)

and *Consumed by You*

(Travis and Cara's romance!)

The Sapphire Affair series...

The Sapphire Affair

The Sapphire Heist

Out of Bounds

A New York Times Bestselling sexy sports romance

The Only One

A second chance love story!

Stud Finder

A sexy, flirty romance!

CONTACT

I love hearing from readers! You can find me on Twitter at LaurenBlakely3, Instagram at LaurenBlakelyBooks, Facebook at LaurenBlakelyBooks, or online at LaurenBlakely.com. You can also email me at laurenblakelybooks@gmail.com

CPSIA information can be obtained
at www.ICGtesting.com
Printed in the USA
LVHW011830011219
639067LV00014B/1049/P

9 781698 382142